HOME

SH

The Rancher by Diana Palmer
Big Sky Standoff by B.J. Daniels
Branded by the Sheriff by Delores Fossen
Texas Lullaby by Tina Leonard
Cowboy for Hire by Marie Ferrarella
Her Rancher Rescuer by Donna Alward

SHIPMENT 2

Last Chance Cowboy by Cathy McDavid
Rancher Rescue by Barb Han
The Texan's Future Bride by Sheri WhiteFeather
A Texan on Her Doorstep by Stella Bagwell
The Rancher's Hired Fiancée by Judy Duarte
That Wild Cowboy by Lenora Worth

SHIPMENT 3

Lone Star Survivor by Colleen Thompson
A Cowboy's Duty by Marin Thomas
Protecting Their Child by Angi Morgan
The Cowboy's Bonus Baby by Tina Leonard
Claimed by a Cowboy by Tanya Michaels
Home to Wyoming by Rebecca Winters
One Brave Cowboy by Kathleen Eagle

SHIPMENT 4

Wearing the Rancher's Ring by Stella Bagwell
The Texas Rancher's Vow by Cathy Gillen Thacker
Wild for the Sheriff by Kathleen O'Brien
A Callahan Wedding by Tina Leonard
Rustling Up Trouble by Delores Fossen
The Cowboy's Family Plan by Judy Duarte

SHIPMENT 5

The Texan's Baby by Donna Alward
Not Just a Cowboy by Caro Carson
Cowboy in the Making by Julie Benson
The Renegade Rancher by Angi Morgan
A Family for Tyler by Angel Smits
The Prodigal Cowboy by Kathleen Eagle

SHIPMENT 6

The Rodeo Man's Daughter by Barbara White Daille
His Texas Wildflower by Stella Bagwell
The Cowboy SEAL by Laura Marie Altom
Montana Sheriff by Marie Ferrarella
A Ranch to Keep by Claire McEwen
A Cowboy's Pride by Pamela Britton
Cowboy Under Siege by Gail Barrett

SHIPMENT 7

Reuniting with the Rancher by Rachel Lee
Rodeo Dreams by Sarah M. Anderson
Beau: Cowboy Protector by Marin Thomas
Texas Stakeout by Virna DePaul
Big City Cowboy by Julie Benson
Remember Me, Cowboy by C.J. Carmichael

SHIPMENT 8

Roping the Rancher by Julie Benson
In a Cowboy's Arms by Rebecca Winters
How to Lasso a Cowboy by Christine Wenger
Betting on the Cowboy by Kathleen O'Brien
Her Cowboy's Christmas Wish by Cathy McDavid
A Kiss on Crimson Ranch by Michelle Major

HOME *on the* RANCH

CLAIMED BY A COWBOY

NEW YORK TIMES BESTSELLING AUTHOR

TANYA MICHAELS

HARLEQUIN® HOME ON THE RANCH

ISBN-13: 978-1-335-45309-9

Claimed by a Cowboy

This edition published by arrangement with Harlequin Books S.A.

For questions and comments about the quality of this book, please contact us at CustomerService@Harlequin.com.

Printed in U.S.A.

Seven-time RITA® Award finalist **Tanya Michaels** is the *New York Times* bestselling author of more than forty books and novellas. Her stories, praised for their poignancy and humor, have received awards from readers and reviewers alike. Tanya lives outside Atlanta with her two teenage children. Together, the three of them watch way too much TV, which Tanya happily justifies as the study of plot arc and characterization.

This book is dedicated to Jane Mims
(what would I do without you?), who graciously
chauffeured me around the Hill Country in spite of
the world's most diabolically uncooperative GPS.

Chapter One

The fifth floor of the insurance company was impressively quiet. Nothing so crass as *noise* leaked from the opulent and distinguished conference rooms at the end of the long corridor—which made junior actuary Lorelei Keller want to cringe at the staccato ccho of her navy pumps against the marble tile. She preferred to stand out in meetings because she possessed a lightning-quick mind, not because everyone could hear her coming from a mile away.

As if her footfalls weren't making her self-conscious enough, the cell phone in her jacket pocket suddenly buzzed. Even with the ringer turned off, the vibration seemed loud in the empty hall. She fished the phone out to check the display screen and scowled. Though no name showed, the 830 area code meant Fredericksburg, Texas. More specifically, her mother. Again.

Exhaling an impatient breath, Lorelei turned the phone off completely and repocketed it. Wanda Keller was her only immediate family and Lorelei loved the woman. But mother and daughter were painfully dissimilar. Graduating from an Ivy League university had been easier for Lorelei than getting through to her mom. *Not that I'm deliberately avoiding her.* She fully intended to call Wanda back later, after business hours. Headed into a meeting with one of the company's top executives was not the time to rehash their argument about Lorelei's refusal to visit at the end of the month.

"You loved Frederick-Fest as a child," Wanda had burbled just two days ago, sounding as enthusiastic as a child herself. She claimed the timing of the weeklong March event would be extra festive this year, since its dates fell over St. Patrick's Day—never mind that their ancestry was German, not Irish—and the spring equinox.

"But I'm not a kid anymore," Lorelei had pointed out as gently as possible. "I have adult responsibilities, like a job I worked hard to get."

"They have to give you vacation time, don't they?" Wanda had persisted.

Lorelei had bit her tongue to keep from saying anything cruel. Like, *I'm not about to use up vacation to come help sell crystals and hand out bookmarks on the protocol for "What to Do if You Encounter a Hill Country Ghost."* "I've got a really busy month ahead of me, Mom."

Wanda's voice, which had been by turns cheerfully cajoling and stubbornly challenging, fell to a barely audible level. "You haven't been home in over a year."

Home. How could Lorelei explain that Texas hadn't felt like home since her father had died twenty years ago? Her freshman year of college, Lorelei had joked with her roommate about "Philadelphia freedom" because moving to Pennsylvania truly had liberated her. She'd been free of living in a house that was a shrine to her dad, free of her mother's increasingly bizarre beliefs. Lorelei had soothed her frazzled nerves with the orderly logic of numbers and let her first snowy

Pennsylvania winter numb a decade of tangled emotions.

"You know I had to cancel at Christmas because I had the flu," Lorelei had defended herself. "I'll come down for a visit this year. I promise."

"When?"

"I don't know, Mom. Soon." Soonish, anyway. "But not this month, okay? I'll look at my calendar, talk to my boss and get back to you."

Her mother had sighed, clearly skeptical. "Sure. I'll be here."

Reaching for the door to the conference room, Lorelei gave a quick shake of her head, her long dark hair swirling about her shoulders, and banished the memory of her impulsive promise. Now was the time to focus on the more pressing topic of risk management. One of the few women in her department, she was determined to distinguish herself among her colleagues. She straightened her spine and stepped into the office, her footsteps now swallowed by the plush carpet. But a last lingering stab of guilt pierced her. *I'll talk to my supervisor tomorrow about vacation time.* Conscience appeased, Lorelei lost herself in the two-hour meeting, all thoughts of Texas and her mother pushed aside.

Lorelei was seated at her desk, immersed in notes for a liability audit, when a male voice said, “Knock knock,” from the doorway. She glanced up to see Rick Caulden.

He flashed a knowing smile. “You forget about me again? Reservations? Tuesday night? Any of this ringing a bell?”

“Of course I remember. I’ve been looking forward to our dinner. I just thought you were going to call when you got here.” She enjoyed her periodic dates with the handsome attorney.

Employed by a law firm several blocks away, Rick worked as hard as she did. He was charming but refreshingly unsentimental. They shared the same pragmatic streak and career drive.

“Tried calling,” he said. “Kept going straight to voice mail, so I decided I should come up, find out if your meeting ran long and if I was on my own for dinner.”

“Oh, right—I turned my phone off before the meeting and totally forgot to turn it back on.” A mistake, or a Freudian slip? Had she deliberately left it off because she suspected

Wanda would call back? Maybe Lorelei had been trying to avoid the guilt trip of feeling like an ungrateful daughter yet again.

As soon as Lorelei repowered the phone, a message bubble appeared. She frowned. "Wow, that's a *lot* of missed calls."

"At least three of them are me," Rick said.

And the other six? "Hang on a sec." She stood, gathering her purse and coat. "I just want to check voice mail before we go."

"Sure." He smirked. "I always make our reservations for fifteen minutes later than I tell you. I know how difficult it is to drag you out of the office."

Under different circumstances, she might have pointed out that she spent an equal amount of time waiting on him or assuring him she didn't mind canceling because he needed the extra time to prepare a motion or speak with a client. Right now, she was more concerned with her messages than Rick's unexpected double standard.

Because of the 830 area code on the missed calls, Lorelei assumed her mother was phoning from one of the hotel lines instead of her private number. But it wasn't Wanda's voice that greeted her.

"Lorelei? I don't know if you remember me, but this is Ava Hirsch."

As if Lorelei had been gone so long she wouldn't recall her mom's best friend? Though Ava's husband was of the vocal opinion that Wanda was "a gallon shy of a keg," the two women had always been inseparable.

"I'm calling..." Ava stopped, sniffed and tried again. "I'm calling about your mother, dear."

At the end of the sentence, Ava's voice broke and the world tilted beneath Lorelei's feet. She groped blindly for her chair.

"Lorelei? What is it?" Rick's concern sounded miles away; Ava's condolences were even more distant, fading beneath the pounding in Lorelei's cars.

But Lorelei didn't need to hear the rest of the message to know. She was going home to Fredericksburg, after all.

Chapter Two

Sam Travis was well-versed in the ghosts of Texas lore—he'd shared many a local legend with tourists around the campfire—but he'd never felt haunted until now.

No matter which room he moved to in the bed-and-breakfast, he still saw his landlady, eccentric Wanda Keller, who had been mothering him on and off for the past three years. *Maybe I should have left with the others.* As of this morning, there had been two other guests staying at the inn. Another proprietor in town had promptly offered them free rooms in light of the tragedy. Wanda had been well-liked in town, even by loners like Sam.

Sam worked multiple seasonal jobs that kept him in motion, but he always circled back to Wanda's, helping her with minor repairs and enjoying her cooking for a week or so before leaving again. It had taken him over a year of just being able to show up, his usual room always vacant, before he'd realized that she held it perpetually open for him. When he'd insisted she shouldn't do that, she'd called him *dummkopf* and responded that it was her inn and she'd do whatever she liked. This B and B, now painfully devoid of her presence, was the closest thing he'd had to a home since the dusty bunkhouse where his uncle had raised him.

But not close enough that he wanted to own the place. He recalled the shock on Ava Hirsch's tear-streaked face that afternoon—it had mirrored his own.

"What do you mean, she *left it to me?*" Too flabbergasted to keep his voice down, Sam had earned angry glares from all the nearby nurses.

Behind her wire-rimmed glasses Ava's eyes had been the size of poker chips. "You didn't know? I never would have said anything. I thought..."

Sitting alone in the dimly lit kitchen hours later, Sam raised his half-finished beer in an affectionate toast. "Still meddling from the great beyond, Wanda?" She'd always nagged him to settle down. If Ava were right about the change to her friend's will—something Sam still didn't quite believe—then maybe it was Wanda's gentle way of coercing him into putting down roots.

He shook his head at the asinine idea of him as a hotel manager. Granted, this was a very small hotel, but that made it worse. Guests expected a personal touch, that extra dose of folksy hospitality. On the trail, in his element, Sam did just fine with tourists as long as they followed his rules about the horses. Most clients who wanted to rough it had a certain expectation of what their guide would be like. His occasionally gruff demeanor fit the part. He didn't have Wanda's gracious nature. The first time some the-customer-is-always-right twit complained about sheet thread count or something equally ridiculous… Well, being raised by a cantankerous bachelor uncle was not the same as attending charm school.

Even though he wouldn't be staying, he was touched by the gesture. If she had bequeathed him the inn, her intentions were good. Wanda may have been trying to give him a home—which was more than his actual mother had ever done—but she seemed to have overlooked that what he'd loved most about the inn was gone. He'd once got jalapeño juice in his eye, and it had burned like hellfire. His dry, unblinking eyes stung far worse now.

"Place won't be the same without her," Sam declared aloud.

A plaintive, otherworldly yowl of agreement came from the floor. Sam nearly jumped until he realized that the reclusive white cat had finally made an appearance—his first all night, although he'd halfheartedly eaten the small plate of food Sam pushed under the bed.

"You miss her, too, don't you?" Sam reached down to scratch Oberon's head, which the cat tolerated for a millisecond before scooting back, his ears flat and his yellow gaze suspicious. The feline had worshipped and adored Wanda Keller, but regarded all other human beings with contempt.

Sam might have made a sarcastic comment, such as telling the cat to have fun opening its own damn can of tuna tomorrow, except he couldn't forget the pet's distress earlier. It had been Oberon who had found Sam in the kitchen and let him know something was wrong, meowing anxiously, tail twitching, constantly glancing back over his shoulder, as if he wanted Sam to follow. Although Wanda normally rose at sunrise to roll out dough for breakfast, Sam had assumed she was sleeping in because of the bad headache she'd mentioned last night. He'd tried to help out by brewing coffee for everyone and putting boxes of cereal around the bowl of fresh fruit on the dining room table.

Sam had followed the cat to her room, but there was nothing to be done. She'd gone in her sleep; the doctors diagnosed a ruptured brain aneurysm. When the paramedics had tried to take the body, Oberon had launched himself at them in hissing attack. Attempts to get hold of the cat had proven futile, and the feline disappeared under Wanda's bed, where he'd begun a low, spine-tingling wail. When Sam had returned from the hospital, Oberon had still been there, his cry hoarser than it had been hours before but just as heartfelt. Sam believed the cat was ornery enough to have tried stalking the ambulance, if Wanda had ever installed a cat door. She worried about him ending up in traffic and getting hit by a tourist watching for street signs.

Now, Oberon sat back on his haunches and studied Sam as if assessing him. The uneven triangle of black fur around the cat's left eye added to his sinister expression. When his slim body tensed to pounce, Sam wondered if he was about to get lacerated for letting them take Wanda away. Instead, the animal shot into Sam's denim-covered lap and circled twice before curling into a warm ball. Sam was shocked, but assumed this was a temporary truce. They were each saying goodbye to the only family they'd had.

We weren't her *only family.* Wanda might have been "like a mom" to him, but she was a real mother to someone else. If there was one thing Wanda had talked about more than her legends, herbs and woo-woo philosophies, it was Lorelei. Sam's jaw tightened. He'd heard dozens of stories about Lorelei, who'd pretended at five that her bicycle was a horse named Spokes and, at ten, had been the first in her class to memorize all the state capitals. Wanda always bragged that Lorelei was as "smart as a whip," which would explain the extra cords and whatnot draped over the young woman's gown in graduation pictures.

Most of the family photos Wanda liked to show off were from back when her husband was alive and Lorelei had been a chubby-cheeked little girl. The most recent portrait he'd seen was from several years ago:

a flinty-eyed, unsmiling college grad who looked just a bit too smug beneath her mortarboard. Wanda had always made excuses for why her pride-and-joy didn't visit. Sam was less inclined to do so.

"Things were hard for her after her dad died," Wanda had said once, looking faraway and sad.

Not wanting to upset his friend, Sam had held his tongue. But he had trouble sympathizing. As a child, he, too, had lost a father. What he'd needed most was comfort from his mother. Instead…

Sam didn't realize he'd been absently petting the cat until he stopped and Oberon butted his head into Sam's arm, protesting.

"Enough of this," Sam told the cat. "You want me to pet you, you have to come with me into the den. No more sitting in the dark, crying into our beer. Metaphorically speaking. Let's see what's on the tube."

He gently set the cat on the floor, and, sure enough, Oberon followed him down the hallway. They passed by a framed picture of Lorelei as a teenager and Sam shook his head. If the woman was so damn smart, why hadn't she known how lucky she was to have Wanda?

* * *

Lorelei was a little surprised that the man behind the counter handed over keys to the rental car. After her sleepless night and turbulent flight into San Antonio this morning, she had deep bags beneath her bloodshot eyes. She probably looked strung out and wouldn't have blamed the guy if he'd insisted on some kind of drug test before letting her drive a car off the lot. Then again, he was already a little scared of her from when she'd growled, "Trust me, I *understand* the optional insurance policy, you can stop overexplaining!" So maybe his thrusting the keys at her was less about customer service and more about getting rid of her.

"Your luggage is already in the trunk," he informed her. "You have a nice day."

Not a chance in hell. "Thank you," she said tightly. She'd been speaking through clenched lips all day; now she gripped the keys so hard they dug into her palm.

It was as if she were trying to hold herself together through sheer physical force because if she didn't, Lorelei might fly apart. She stalked across the lot toward her assigned car, barely giving herself a moment to buckle in and adjust the seat and mirrors before heading for the exit. If she paused to consult a map, paused to find a radio station, paused for one second to think…

Although it had been a while since her last trip here—*I'm sorry, Mom. I will always be sorry*—she knew the I-10 route by heart. There were no surprise detours this Wednesday afternoon. The city gave way to unmanicured vistas, tree-studded hills and pastures that looked furry due to bunches of some tawny untamed grass.

About fifteen minutes from Fredericksburg, she stopped at a filling station to use their restroom even though it wasn't really necessary. Maybe she was just stalling because she couldn't face what awaited her.

It was surprisingly warm outside—she'd dressed that morning for March in Philly, not March in Texas. On her drive, she'd already seen a few patches of bluebonnets in bloom. Wanda had loved plants of all kinds. Lorelei had a stray memory of a picnic with her parents, long ago, in a field of wildflowers. Her mother had told her a Native American legend about how flowers had become fragrant. Wanda had grown plants both decorative and functional in window boxes and pots all through their house and yard. She and her husband had turned to medicinal herbs and holistic treatments when he was diagnosed with liver cancer, rather than to oncologists.

With a hard swallow, Lorelei climbed back into the rental car, annoyed with herself for postponing the inevitable. She could stop every mile between here and the bed-and-breakfast and it wouldn't change anything. *I've lost them both.*

When she'd called Ava last night with her flight details, Ava had volunteered her husband, Clinton, to come pick up Lorelei in San Antonio. "If you insist on driving yourself, at least call us when you get close. We'll meet you at the B and B."

Lorelei had thanked the woman sincerely for the offer but had said she'd call them later because she might want a nap before seeing anyone. It had been a half truth. There was no way she'd be able to sleep, but she needed to be alone in her mother's inn. Being there would solidify the loss and Lorelei wasn't sure how much longer she could keep from detonating. The last thing she wanted was a witness.

Though she had to slow down temporarily for a stretch of road where signs warned Loose Livestock, she didn't encounter traffic.

Judging from the wry sign on a dilapidated diner—Over a Dozen Served!—she was officially on the road less traveled. All too soon, she was turning onto the street where the Haunted Hill Country Bed-and-Breakfast sat.

Lorelei parked the car in front of the stone-faced two-story building, bracing herself for not hearing her mother's voice when she walked inside. Would she still smell the uniquely familiar blend of lemon, lavender and nutmeg from the incenses and oils Wanda had favored? Those aromatherapy scents had permeated the entire inn. Except during Christmas seasons when the bed-and-breakfast was filled with fresh pine and baking gingerbread.

"Get out of the car," Lorelei muttered. If she sat in the driveway much longer, some kind passerby would stop to tell her that the B and B wasn't currently open for business, that the owner had…

She wrenched open the door, then crossed the short sidewalk leading to the porch. The front steps creaked softly beneath her weight, and she was attempting to fish the key from her purse when the door swung open.

A tall man in a plaid button-down shirt

and a cowboy hat greeted her. "Sorry, we're not— Ah. It's you."

She drew herself up straighter, the involuntary reflex making her feel a touch juvenile. Even if she stood on tippy-toe, she wouldn't be level with him. He was at least six feet. "I'm L—"

"Oh, I know who you are," he interrupted in a lazy drawl. He rocked back on his heels, seemingly in no hurry to move the hell out of her way so she could lock herself in a bedroom and have a private breakdown. Not that indulging in an emotional fit would bring her mother back.

"You're little Lori," he continued, thumbs hooked in the front pockets of his jeans. "Wanda's girl, all grown up."

She almost snapped that she wasn't anyone's "little" anything. She was five foot eight for crying out loud! And what was with the *all-grown-up* condescension? He looked three or four years older, tops. "I go by Lorelei. No one's ever called me Lori, particularly not total strangers who block doorways." She glared meaningfully.

He glared back.

"So who are you?" she demanded. "An employee?"

"Not exactly." Hardly an informative answer, but at least he stepped to the side.

"Ava told me all the guests were relocated," she said as she crossed the threshold into the foyer. A cursory glance at the adjacent dining room and den showed that everything was as she remembered—except for her mom's absence and this annoying man's presence. "I had expected to be alone."

The man shrugged. "Someone had to take care of Oberon."

How could she have forgotten the maniacal cat? As a scraggly kitten, Oberon had shown up on the front porch while Wanda and the real estate agent had been doing a walk-through of the inn.

"He was a sign," Wanda had told her daughter over the phone. "I was meant to buy this place, and he was meant to keep me company. It's been so lonely with your father gone and you at college."

"Ow!" A sudden scratch to the ankle jolted Lorelei back to the present, and she bumped the *willkommen* table. Brochures detailing area activities sat alongside the guestbook and one pamphlet fell to the floor. A telltale white paw jutted out from beneath the tablecloth. *Speak of the freaking devil.*

Grimacing, she took a large step away from the table and, more importantly, the extended claws. "I see Oberon hasn't mellowed with age."

"Nope."

She suppressed a sigh at the man's flat tone. Good thing he was attractive; he'd be doomed if all he had going for him was personality. *Attractive?* That must be the sleep deprivation talking. While she couldn't find fault with the cowboy's well-muscled body—and his green eyes were admittedly arresting—he was a bit scruffy with his too-long dark golden hair and the stubble dotting his jawline. Not her type at all.

"I assume you have a name?" she prompted.

He flashed a mocking smile that lasted just long enough to reveal deep dimples. "Good assumption. Now, if you'll excuse me, Miz Keller, I was on my way out. Help yourself to any room except the Faust suite. That's mine."

As in, he would be sleeping there? She'd hoped he was only dropping by to feed the cat. "You'll be back tonight?"

"Yes, ma'am." He must have caught the dismay in her expression because his eyes narrowed. "Don't worry, this place is plenty big enough for both of us."

Despite the multiple bedrooms in the two-floor structure, she didn't believe him. And she couldn't help noticing he didn't seem convinced, either.

The door banged shut in Sam's wake as he strode toward the truck parked behind the inn. He wanted to leave quickly, before the B and B's omnipresent reminders of Wanda nettled his conscience like the spines of a prickly pear cactus. She would have wanted him to be more welcoming to her daughter. *Hard to believe they're related.*

He'd known from pictures that Lorelei was dark-haired and striking. He just hadn't realized she was so tall; her mama had been a round little dumpling of a woman. Other than her height, though, Lorelei Keller had been pretty much what he'd expected. Purse-lipped and haughty, with no mention of her mother. Granted, Lorelei's dark eyes had been puffy, but no more than most tourists' in pollen season.

He could almost hear his former landlady's chiding voice. *Oh, and you were a real charmer during that encounter? You didn't even give her a chance.* With a sigh, he glanced back over his shoulder, then retraced his steps.

Through the window in the door, he could see the brunette slumped in a chair at the kitchen table, much the same way he'd been last night. As soon as he turned the knob, her backbone went ramrod straight. Her expensive-looking cinnamon-colored sweater dress was probably hot and itchy on a day like this. Over it, she wore some kind of full-body vest in an even darker brown. In contrast, he couldn't help recalling the way Wanda had cheerfully embraced colors—the brighter, the better.

"Forget something?" Lorelei asked without turning to look at him.

"Just wanted to say, name's Sam Travis. I was a good friend of your mother's. Damn fine woman." He paused a beat, to see if Lorelei recognized his name or had any comment. Did she know what Ava suspected, that Wanda had altered her will in the past year? "I'm the one who found her. Yesterday."

Red-rimmed eyes met his, and Lorelei swallowed, struggling to speak. "Do you think she was in pain?"

"She complained of a headache when she went to bed the night before, but no, I don't think she suffered. Doc Singer made it sound as if it was about as peaceful as passing can be."

Lorelei drew in a shaky breath. "Thank you, Sam."

He nodded uncomfortably. "I won't be back for a couple of hours, but is there anything I can bring you from town? Anything you need?"

Her gaze clashed with his, naked and vulnerable. For a split second, all he saw was need. Then she blinked, eradicating the defenselessness so fast he could pretend he'd imagined it.

"That won't be necessary," she said. "But I appreciate the offer. By the way, I've decided to take the wolf suite."

The one farthest in the house from his.

Good. Maybe they would only bump into each other a minimum of times before the memorial service on Saturday.

He knew from Wanda's lawyer that the reading of the will would follow—Wanda's way of making sure that on the same day her loved ones were honoring her, she'd get to express her love for them—and Sam's attendance was requested. Considering how much Wanda had adored her prodigal daughter, would she really have left Sam the inn?

And what the hell was he going to do with it if she had?

Chapter Three

Lorelei hung up the phone with a sigh and glanced across the kitchen. Ava was stocking the refrigerator with all manner of casseroles and comfort foods. Judging by the dozens of containers she'd arrived with an hour ago, she'd been cooking nonstop since yesterday.

"That was the last one," Lorelei said wearily. She'd gone through her mom's reservation file at the computer and called to cancel all the guests scheduled for the following week. After that… Well, surviving this week was the first step.

Lorelei didn't really know what she would do about the inn. She supposed hiring someone to manage it for her was a possibility, but she'd never really warmed to this place. When her mother—who'd worked previous jobs as a cook in another hotel and an administrative assistant in the town tourism bureau—first said she wanted to open her own inn, Lorelei had thought it would be a good fit for her, assuming Wanda could get the necessary loans. Ever since her husband's death, Wanda had slipped into more and more elaborate flights of fancy. She used to wake Lorelei up in the middle of the night to excitedly tell her, "Your daddy visited me again. He's watching over us, honey, and he's real proud of you." Lorelei had wanted to shake her, had wanted to yell at her mother to stop it. It was so hard to let go and heal when Wanda kept his specter alive and well in their home. Lorelei had foolishly presumed that running a business would keep Wanda more grounded.

Should've known better. There were lots of bed-and-breakfasts and guest ranches dotting the Hill Country. Wanda had tried to set hers apart with its theme. Her place served as sort of a museum for Hill Country folklore and ghost stories. Each guest room was based on some local legend.

For instance, Lorelei's room, from the

comforter printed with running wolves to the hand-carved figures on the wooden vanity, centered on the wolf spirit that "haunted" nearby Devil's Backbone, an area also rumored to host the apparitions of monks, Native Americans and Confederate soldiers. Sam's suite was based on the famed Faust Hotel, a historic haunted site, and Wanda had decorated it based on old photos she'd seen of the establishment. The only creepy room was the one based on a cave, in which Wanda had blacked out the windows and bat noises played periodically through a hidden speaker. In addition to the themed decorating, Wanda had also arranged tours that took visitors through the region from one "unexplained phenomenon" to another. And Wanda had always been a hell of a storyteller, probably because she believed the outlandish tales she shared.

"She'll be missed," one of the scheduled guests had told Lorelei, choked up by the news that the inn's proprietor had died. "My husband and I came to the Haunted Hill Country every year for our anniversary, and we just loved Wanda. Your mother was a special woman."

Ava came toward her with two cups of coffee. "You look like you could use some." Then she reached into a cabinet beneath the counter and procured a bottle of whiskey. "And maybe a shot of this with it."

Lorelei gave a dry laugh. She wasn't much of a drinker, but she appreciated the thought. "Thanks, Ava."

"Least I can do." Ava slid her glasses up on her nose with a finger. "I wish you had let me help with those calls. You didn't have to take care of them alone. Can't be easy to tell people over and over that your mama's gone."

"I wanted to." Saying it forced her to accept it. Running from the truth wouldn't change it. "I needed to be doing something, keeping busy."

Ava cast a sheepish look over her shoulder, at the crammed full refrigerator. "Guess I can understand that."

Lorelei poured a modest token shot into her coffee and raised her eyebrows questioningly at Ava, who nodded and pushed her own mug across the counter.

"Hit me, barkeep." Ava waited for her own more generous slug, then stirred cream into both mugs with a cinnamon stick.

Lorelei inhaled deeply. Her mug smelled like heaven. "Ava, can I ask you a...delicate question?"

The older woman nodded, her faded grey

eyes earnest. "I know we haven't seen much of each other in the years since you got your degree, but Wanda was the closest thing I ever had to a sister. I'd be honored if you thought of me as kin."

"Was there something romantic going on between Mom and Sam Travis?"

Ava spluttered, choking on coffee.

"Sorry." Lorelei handed her a couple of napkins, feeling guilty as Ava continued to cough.

"What a thing to suggest!" Ava finally managed to say, cream dotting her upper lip. "Of course there wasn't anything romantic. Thank God you asked me and not Sam. He'd be horrified."

Lorelei's face grew hot. Now that she'd voiced the question, it did sound absurd—especially given how devoted Wanda had remained to her late husband. "Well, I didn't think so, but I wanted to be sure. It's not like she was always conventional with her beliefs, so she might have overlooked the age difference. He was cryptic and grudging. All he told me was that they were 'good friends.' But he'd obviously talked to her right before she went to sleep and he was the one who found her in her bed."

Had Sam Travis been the person to hear her mother's final words?

Lorelei couldn't help flinching, recalling her mom's last words the last time they'd spoken. *I'll be here.* The mug trembled in Lorelei's hands. She'd taken for granted that her mother would, indeed, always be here.

She cleared her throat. "The biggest reason I wondered about their relationship is because of you."

"Me?" Ava squeaked.

"Well, you didn't mention him to me when we spoke on the phone and you said all the guests had gone." A heads-up that someone else was going to be under the same roof with her would have been nice. "But every time he's come up in conversation this afternoon, you've..."

Ava turned away, busying herself with a rag and wiping down the long expanse of already clean counter.

"You're acting weird about Sam." Almost guilty, which had made Lorelei speculate that maybe Ava harbored a secret about her mom and the cowboy. *Something* was clearly bothering Ava.

"Is there anything you want to tell me?" Lorelei prodded.

"Only that it's wonderful to see you again." Ava put the rag down and smiled sadly. "I just wish you could have come home before this." There was no accusation in her voice, but that made it even worse somehow.

Lorelei was tempted to agree with Ava, to say *I wish I had, too,* but Lorelei had given up wishing a long time ago. When her dad died, she'd wised up—no wishing wells or "first star I see tonight" or fairy stories for her. Those were all just pretty guises for denial. Lorelei needed to live in cold, hard reality. And that meant she knew what to do with the inn.

She'd sell the property and use the money to help with her staggering college loans. Wanda would approve. Her mother had been proud that Lorelei got into such a prestigious school and she'd always fretted that she couldn't do more to take care of her daughter from so far away. The woman who'd once given her crystals and dream catchers for protection would be assisting in protection from debt, a far more useful security. It was something tangible and *parental* Wanda could do for her, which made Lorelei feel, for a moment, closer to the mother she'd lost.

Lorelei bit her lip, wondering if she should tell Ava what she intended to do. But it seemed cruel just now, with the inn being the most visible reminder of Wanda. Lorelei didn't want the kind-hearted woman to feel as if she was losing her friend twice in one week. *I'll tell her after the memorial service Saturday.*

With the decision made to sell, Lorelei felt as if she could breathe easier. As an adolescent, grieving for her father, she'd hoped that they could move away, start fresh somewhere his memory wasn't so potent. At the very least, she'd wanted Wanda to date, to set the example that it wasn't a betrayal to move on with life. Instead, Wanda had continued to talk about him as if he were a member of their household. On holidays and special occasions, she set a place for him at the table. She talked about having spirit conversations with him in her dreams and seeing his ghost in his favorite recliner. The lack of closure had ripped at Lorelei.

Not this time. After the service and the will-reading, when she officially inherited the inn, she'd call the would-be guests in her mom's files and break the news to them. She'd sell the B and B to someone who could create their own niche here, and she'd return to her life in Philly, her ties to Fredericksburg severed. Lorelei would have the closure she so desperately needed.

* * *

Sitting in the middle of a semi-circle of pictures, Lorelei debated opening a window. *It's stuffy in here.* Given the high ceiling of the great room and the dropping evening temperatures, she knew the stifling sensation was in her imagination. Raising a window would be yielding to her sudden illogical claustrophobia. Lorelei was a pragmatic woman. She refused to start acting squirrelly just because it was late and she was all alone in the inn.

Sam's estimated "couple of hours" of being gone had turned into all afternoon and evening. Ava had insisted on staying long enough to have dinner with Lorelei but then had returned home to her husband. Both women had listlessly pushed their food around on Wanda's sunset-colored ceramic plates. During the meal, Ava had tentatively broached the subject of the eulogy Lorelei needed to write for Saturday's memorial. There was also the task of selecting pictures for display at the funeral home. A salon decorated with mementos of Wanda Keller's life would open an hour prior to the formal service so that loved ones could gather to share their recollections. And their grief.

The service would take place there at the

funeral home. Wanda, never really a church-going woman, had decided against having her final farewell at one of the local chapels. Since she was being cremated, like her husband before her, there would be no graveyard burial, either.

Lorelei shoved her hands through her hair. Her first attempt at drafting a eulogy had been disastrous. She'd thought that pulling out all these old photos, conjuring the memories, would help organize her thoughts. Sort of like an outline for a college paper. But seeing her mother's life, now ended, spread out on the carpet around her…

A jagged keening broke the silence, and she pressed her fist against her mouth, trying to stem the dark wave of despair. Though she was usually comfortable with solitude, right now the overpowering sense of aloneness choked her. She gripped her cell phone, wanting to escape by talking to someone outside of Fredericksburg. But it was too late to call any of her work friends back in Philly, especially given the time difference. Rick, maybe?

No. She recalled with a grimace his distant response when she'd learned of her mother's death. He'd said he was sorry, naturally, had even offered the rote "if there's anything I can do..." But he'd sounded more like a lawyer giving a client bad news than a potential lover. "Can I send flowers?" he'd asked. "Or was she one of those people who'd prefer a donation to charity, in lieu of?"

A metallic jiggling cut through Lorelei's thoughts and she stiffened. The B and B had never seemed creepier than it did at that moment.

Once she realized that what she'd heard was the back door being unlocked, she expelled a shaky breath. *Sam.* When they'd met earlier today, all she'd wanted was for him to get the hell out. Tonight, though, she was grateful for his presence. She almost called out to him but bit her lip, embarrassed by her neediness. He'd come through here anyway to get to his suite.

Sure enough, a moment later, booted footsteps sounded in the short, hardwood hallway leading from the kitchen. Then Sam appeared at the edge of the spacious living room, his face shadowed by his cowboy hat and the dark hall. It probably would have been better for her nerves if she'd turned on more lights than the standing fixture in the corner and a stained-glass antique table lamp.

She felt exposed in her circle of photos and

muted light. The fact that she was wearing a tank top and flannel pajama bottoms didn't help. "Hi."

He leaned against the wall, seeming caught by all the images of Wanda. "Can't believe she's gone." His quiet murmur didn't completely mask the emotion in his voice. Once again, Lorelei wondered how Sam and her mother had met and what their relationship had been. It was easy to picture Wanda and Ava as best friends, laughing over botched recipes and antiquing together on the weekend. But what had Sam and Wanda shared?

"I'm supposed to pick photos for the funeral home," she told him, her voice cracking only the slightest bit when she said *funeral.*

"Would you like to know which ones were her favorites?" Sam offered.

Her erstwhile relief at his company crisped and blackened to irritation. "I'm her daughter," she said defensively. "You don't think I can figure that out for myself?"

He tipped his hat back with a finger, staring her down with those green eyes.

"You think you knew her better than I did," Lorelei said.

He somehow shrugged without ever moving his shoulders. "Even when we suppose we know someone, we can be surprised. But I did spend some time with her."

And I didn't spend nearly enough. Guilt clogged Lorelei's windpipe, making it impossible to speak.

"She dragged out her box of photos plenty," he said. "Made me look at them so she could talk about her husband. Or brag about you."

Lorelei wanted so badly to ask what her mother had said. How had she described the brainy, estranged daughter who had so little in common with her?

Sam straightened slowly, awkwardly, and it was only as he moved away from the wall that she realized he was unsteady. Come to think of it, was his drawl more pronounced than it had been that afternoon?

"You've been drinking!"

"Not uncommon in these parts to honor a person's memory by hoisting a glass." He paused. "Can't say I recall the exact number of glasses, but that's why I walked. Left my truck at the bar."

A strange shiver pulsed through her. She was alone in this large house with a broad-shouldered cowboy she barely knew and he might be inebriated. Should she be concerned for her welfare? Wanda had apparently believed in him, but then Wanda had believed a lot of things.

Sam approached, and Lorelei felt the instinct to scoot back, except there wasn't much room behind her. She was between the ring of pictures and the bottom edge of the sofa. When he crouched down, Lorelei breathed in a subtle blend of denim, soap, beer and the crisp March night. It was unexpected. Rick always smelled like designer cologne—appealing, in a manufactured way, but indistinct from dozens of other successful men.

Sam Travis was distinct.

Looking into his eyes, she couldn't remember having ever seen a pair like them. "Wh-what are you doing?"

"Helping."

"I didn't ask for your help." It felt invasive, having him loom over these snapshots of her life. The too-short era when her mother and father were both alive, the later pictures of a smiling Wanda and tense adolescent Lorelei.

Sam's jaw clenched. "Maybe I'm helping *her.* You'll probably pick out the most formal portraits in the bunch, regardless of how Wanda would want to be remembered."

"That's not true. I'm aware of how different my mother and I are. Were."

A fuzzy photo that predated the age of clear digital prints caught her eye, this one of a blurry Wanda laughing with tourists at a festival booth. She had thrived on the conversation and merriment around her. At the edge of the picture was a dark-haired smudge. *Me.* Though it was difficult to tell from the shot, Lorelei had been huddled in a lawn chair with her nose in a book. For all that Lorelei had excelled in school, she'd always had the feeling that her free-spirited mother, who held no degree of her own, would have been more proud if her daughter had put the books down and just enjoyed the sunshine and crowds more.

Sam rocked back on his heels. "Sorry. You're right, this isn't my place." He stood, exiting the room with efficient speed and purpose despite however many glasses he'd drunk in Wanda's memory.

Lorelei bit her bottom lip hard, staring at the mix of antiques and fanciful touches in this central Texas bed-and-breakfast, none of which spoke to Lorelei or resembled her life in Philly. An all too familiar bubble of alienation surrounded her. *It's not my place, either.*

Thursday night, Sam stepped into the kitchen as gingerly as a prowler trying to pass through the house unnoticed. He'd grabbed a burger in town a couple of hours ago, but judging by the angry meow that had greeted Sam as soon as he set foot inside, Oberon had not yet eaten dinner. *At least he has his appetite back.*

Now that Sam was moving in the direction of the cat food, Oberon trilled his approval and wound figure eights between Sam's cowboy boots, nearly tripping him. "You know," he whispered, "you'll get fed a lot faster if you don't knock me on my ass."

The tiptoeing and whispering was embarrassing—but preferable to another charged encounter with Lorelei Keller. Last night, a number of folks in town had been commiserating over Wanda's death; though Sam wasn't usually much of a joiner, he'd ended up drinking with them before walking back to the inn. The sight of Lorelei in the middle of the living room had surprised him. She'd looked like a completely different woman with her arms and shoulders bared in a thin tank top, her long dark hair cascading over her skin.

Or maybe it was the play of vulnerability across her face that had changed her appearance. At any rate, it hadn't taken him long to realize he was intruding on her grief. He didn't want to make the same mistake twice, especially on a night when he was bone sore and smelled like horse. He'd spent the day several towns over, helping a friend train an Arabian.

Suddenly a woman's agitated voice cut through the silence. "Yes, but I'm telling you, that's not necessary!" After that brief outburst, her voice trailed off some—he could only make out the words *information* and *tomorrow.* Whatever Lorelei was feeling in the wake of her mom's death, he'd been wrong to imagine she was fragile and weepy. Even through a closed door, Sam could hear the steel in her voice.

"She's about as warm and fuzzy as you are," he told the cat, scooping canned food onto a small mound of kibble. Sam was just placing the plastic bowl in the floor when light flooded the kitchen. He blinked at the sudden illumination.

Lorelei gasped in the doorway, one hand flattened over her chest. Along with a pair of jeans, she was wearing another sweater that seemed too thick for Texas. "Jeez. What are you doing skulking in the dark? You scared the hell out of me."

Sam glared. No way was he admitting he'd been sneaking around, trying to make himself as invisible as possible, out of respect to her. "I just came in to feed the cat. Someone should," he said pointedly.

Her lip curled. "I don't think vamp-cat wants pet store food. He's after fresh blood. After trying to take a chunk from my leg yesterday, he lacerated my arm this afternoon when I stopped him from running out the front door."

"Starving an animal does tend to make it mean." He didn't share that he himself had once suggested that Lucifer would be a more appropriate name for the animal.

Lorelei sighed. "You're probably right. Not that he wasn't mean to begin with, but I was negligent, forgetting to feed him. I suppose there's a litter box around here somewhere, too?" She made a face. "I'm not used to taking care of anything."

"Yeah, you don't seem like the pet-owner type."

She narrowed her eyes but didn't argue. Instead, she sidestepped him. "I just came in here to get a drink. I'll be out of your way in no time." When she opened the fridge to retrieve a gallon of lemonade, he saw the mountain of food Ava had stocked was virtually untouched.

"You eat any dinner?" he heard himself ask awkwardly. Stupid question. *She's a grown woman, not the cat. She can feed herself when she chooses.*

"Actually, no." Lorelei sounded bemused by the realization. "Guess I forgot. I've been working all evening."

"Working? Surely your bosses don't expect you to be on call two days before your mother's memorial service?" Sam had worked for a few hard-hearted SOBs in his time, but they'd all understood stopping to remember the dead.

"It was my choice. And my business."

Right—so butt out, cowboy. Message received loud and clear.

He tipped his hat to her. "Good night then, Miss Keller. Oh, but before I forget." Bending to the cabinet beneath the sink, he retrieved a small trash bag and a slotted plastic scooper. "Here. Cat box is in the sunroom."

Lorelei's fingers shook as she unlocked the back door on Friday morning. In order to pull out her keys, she'd had to set down the cardboard flat she'd carried. The thought of picking it back up didn't help her trembling. What she wouldn't give to be in her office right now.

The desperate thought conjured an image

of Sam's disapproving expression last night. No doubt he considered her an unfeeling ice-queen for obsessing over work at a time like this. Not that she gave a damn about his opinion.

Her job was soothing. Numbers and facts and statistics—they'd always lulled her out of anxiety. Wasn't that why people were supposed to count sheep? Unfortunately, being an actuary wasn't really a work-from-home kind of career. She'd prevaricated yesterday. Her hours spent on the phone hadn't been so much working as turning her projects over to two other junior actuaries at the company. Her supervisor had insisted.

"Take a couple of weeks off," he'd told her. "You haven't used a single vacation day in what, over a year? You need it. And we need you at one hundred percent. You're officially on sabbatical."

Tears stung her eyes. What her boss saw as sabbatical, she saw as exile from the only thing that might keep her sane through the next few days. Today had been awful, and she still had the memorial service and an obligatory meeting with her mom's lawyer tomorrow.

Maybe I should have let Ava come with me this morning. The older woman had offered, but Lorelei had suspected her mother's friend would dissolve into tears, threatening Lorelei's own composure. Taking a deep breath, she carried the open-topped box inside and set it gingerly on the counter. The green-and-azure urn that rose from within was porcelain, decorated with bluebonnets and Indian paintbrush. Objectively, Lorelei had to admit it was a lovely container. Wanda had selected it to coordinate with her late husband's urn, which bore a picture of a pecan tree.

Hysteria rose inside of Lorelei and erupted as a horrified giggle. *Oh, God. This is all that's left of my family—matching vases.*

Reflexively, she reached into her pocket for her cell phone. She could call Celia, see how the policy presentation—which had been Lorelei's and had now changed hands—was going. Part of Lorelei acknowledged that she was micromanaging a peer and that she was undoubtedly annoying Celia with her offers to answer questions or to email additional background information. As she dialed, she promised herself she'd do something to make it up to the other woman when she returned to Philadelphia. For now, Lorelei just needed to survive the next forty-eight hours.

Chapter Four

Picturesque clouds dotted an impossibly blue sky, uninterrupted by air traffic or hazy pollution—only the occasional songbird in flight. The sun shone, but gently enough that no one broke a sweat, even in black mourning attire or a suit jacket. It was the afternoon every bride would want for her wedding.

Well, except for Wanda, who'd once claimed that she'd been "delighted" it rained during her long-ago September wedding and had in fact been hoping for a downpour. She held with the superstition that rain on a wedding day meant good luck. Another tradition she'd embraced was the prewedding *Poltera-*

bend. Many dishes had been broken in hopes of bringing luck to the happy couple.

Lorelei's throat tightened as she thought of pictures she'd seen of her parents' wedding day. They'd been so young and in love! Neither of them had been old enough to die. Yet here Lorelei was once again at a family-owned funeral home that had been part of the community for a hundred years, entering through the same white columns she'd passed through on the day of her father's memorial service.

One of the brothers who ran the place was at her side immediately, murmuring his condolences and ushering her to the salon where her mother was being honored today. They'd done a lovely job displaying portraits amid floral arrangements, but the overpowering scent of so many competing flowers in a closed space made Lorelei's nose twitch and irritated her eyes.

Ava and her husband arrived first, immediately followed by other people who had adored Wanda. A crowd gathered around Lorelei, men and women anxious to share their memories of her mother. All around her, the town's citizens regaled each other with stories. The room took on a buzz that made her feel as if she were trapped in a beehive. Lorelei knew her mom had been a very gracious person, could remember the comfort Wanda had taken in those close to her when her husband had passed. Wanda had laughed with them, cried with them and hugged everyone.

In contrast, Lorelei seemed to stiffen at contact. After thirty minutes, her head throbbed. She kept eyeing the door, wanting to escape and steal a few moments of peace for herself before the official service began.

Halfway through yet another recollection from the head librarian, a woman who had helped Wanda do folklore research for the B and B, Lorelei finally interrupted. "I'm sorry," she said, placing a conciliatory hand on the woman's arm. "If you'll please excuse me for a moment, I just need..." *To get the hell out of here.* Luckily, the circumstances didn't require an excuse. The small circle of people who'd gathered around her nodded sympathetically and immediately broke formation so she could pass.

Lorelei went as quickly as decorum allowed toward a side door that led into the employee parking lot. She figured there was less risk that way for running into anyone. The service started in fifteen minutes, and there might still be mourners arriving through the front door.

She stepped outside, lifted her face to the breeze and inhaled deeply when the door shut, muffling the conversations she'd left behind.

"How're you holding up?"

Whipping her head around, she spotted Sam Travis. He was perched on the ramp railing that ran the length of the building. She'd seen him earlier—without his cowboy hat, for once—talking to Clinton and Ava Hirsch, and she'd been relieved when he didn't approach her. Sam made her...uneasy, a sensation she hadn't experienced in a long time.

By the end of elementary school, she'd known she didn't fit in with other kids. They labeled her a math geek and didn't invite her to the giggly slumber parties her female classmates later rehashed in the cafeteria. She'd told herself it didn't matter. At thirteen, she'd decided she was getting out of town as soon as possible. In college, she'd bonded with students similar to her and had been comfortable in her own skin ever since. She knew who she was and what she wanted out of life. She made sensible decisions, such as dating eminently compatible men and not wearing ridiculously high-heeled shoes that could injure her joints or back.

But something about Sam made her feel as if she were teetering even in her practical pumps. She swallowed. "Wh-what are you doing out here?"

"Same thing as you. Hiding."

She bristled at the implied cowardice. "I'm not 'hiding,' Mr. Travis. I just—"

"Easy, darlin'. I wasn't criticizing. There are a lot of very emotional, very *talkative* people in that building. Enough to make anyone skittish." He shook his head. "Not that Wanda would have bolted. She was damn good at listening to everyone, making them feel welcome. Special."

Lorelei was torn. She knew what he meant, yet how many times growing up had she tried to explain to her mother how she felt? How often had Lorelei retreated to her room, frustrated that her mother *wouldn't* listen?

"I've always felt so removed from her," Lorelei heard herself admit. She wasn't sure why she was confiding in him, but she'd be gone soon—back to her real life—so what did it matter? "I tried telling myself I take after Dad, but I don't think it's true. He and Mom were like two peas in a pod, and I was, I don't know, some kind of changeling baby." Of all the crazy legends her mom had ever voiced, that one Lorelei could have believed.

Sam squinted at her from his spot in the shade. "You were how old when you lost your dad?"

"Six when he was diagnosed, seven when he died."

"I was nine when I lost my father. I don't know about you, but a lot of the memories I have are hazy. Maybe you're more like him than you recall."

There he went again, knocking her off balance. She hadn't expected him to try to comfort her. Nor had she expected them to have anything in common. She wondered how he'd lost his own father, if the tragedy had brought Sam and his mother closer.

"I should go back inside," she said, unenthusiastic about the prospect. "The service will be starting soon." The hours she'd spent working on the eulogy had been grueling, but she didn't back down from a challenge.

Sam nodded. "I'll be along in a minute. You look real nice, by the way."

Could he guess how many times she'd changed, trying to decide the right thing to wear? The navy-and-yellow print sheath dress allowed her to wear the big bright yellow earrings her mom had sent for her birthday; the cropped navy blazer helped subdue the outfit enough for the occasion.

Wanting to downplay the way she'd overanalyzed her decision, she made light of Sam's compliment, keeping her voice wry enough that he wouldn't take her seriously. "I don't think it's appropriate to flirt with the deceased's daughter."

He rolled his eyes. "I just meant it's good to see you wearing some color. She would have liked that."

"Says the man in head-to-toe black?" She doubted Sam owned a suit. Today he was showing respect in black boots, crisp jeans that looked starched to within an inch of their life and a black button-down shirt that was a dramatic foil to his light hair and eyes.

"Well." His expression didn't change, but there was a grin in his voice. "I had planned to accessorize with yellow, too, but I couldn't find my headband."

Lorelei laughed before she could stop herself. "I'll see you inside. And thank you."

He inclined his head in a silent "you're welcome," and she turned to go. When she'd fled the guests in the building, her body had been rigid with tension. Now, though far from relaxed, she felt calm enough to deliver her mother's eulogy. How had a virtual stranger Lorelei didn't especially like known what to say? He'd even made her laugh, which was a hell of a feat on this particular occasion.

Lorelei still didn't have the whole story on how Sam and Wanda had become friends, but she understood how much her flamboyant mother had appreciated people who were unpredictable. And Sam Travis was full of surprises.

The barrage of mourners and conversation didn't stop after the memorial service; it followed Lorelei back to the inn. She would forever be grateful to local B and B owners Clare Theo and Bertha Hoffman—women who'd respected Wanda enough to want to honor her without being so close to her that they were overcome with their own grief. They took point on making gallons of coffee and splitting hostess duties, managing the flow of traffic through the downstairs rooms.

Though his truck was in its customary spot out back, Lorelei hadn't spotted Sam in the throng. Was he avoiding the crowd, sequestered away in his room, or was he in this crush somewhere? People kept coming up to hug her and present her with foil-covered dishes. She had enough king ranch casseroles and pecan pies to last until summer. Thank God her mother had purchased a deep freeze, because the refrigerator was long past full.

"Lorelei?" Ava's voice broke through the hum of surrounding conversations. "Lorelei, dear?"

Lorelei glanced over a petite blonde who'd been extolling the virtues of cheddar mashed potatoes as comfort food and saw Ava totter into the formal dining room, wobbling on fancy shoes and too little sleep. Lorelei thanked the guest whose name she'd never quite caught and met Ava in the center of the room.

"I'm glad to see a friendly face," Lorelei said. "This is all a bit…overwhelming."

"Let's go upstairs," Ava suggested. She hesitated before adding, "The lawyer's ready for us."

Lorelei had met Robert Stork earlier in the week when he'd come by with a fruit basket to offer his condolences. He was a sandy-haired man with a round face that made him look barely old enough to drive. She'd been startled when he first introduced himself.

"But Mr. Stork is a white-haired man shorter than I am," she'd blurted, remembering the attorney from her dad's death.

"You're thinking of my father, for whom I'm named," Robert the younger had said. "He's retired and plays a lot of golf now. I took over the family business."

And part of Stork Jr.'s business was to go over Wanda's last wishes with Lorelei and Ava.

Lorelei took a deep breath, steadying herself. "Lead the way."

Instead of going up the steps at the front of the house where all the guests were, the two women detoured to the laundry room and took the narrow spiral of back stairs. *Library* was a rather pretentious term for what Lorelei suspected had once been a generously sized walk-in closet. The cramped area was furnished with four chairs too close together for personal space and built-in shelves, probably meant for linens but now filled with books. Still, the tiny room had the advantage of being removed from the nonstop conversation and parade of food on the first floor.

Just before they reached the room, Ava paused, twisting the slim gold bracelets on her wrist.

"What is it?" Lorelei asked. For obvious reasons, Ava hadn't been very jovial today. Yet now her expression seemed particularly troubled.

"I…nothing, dear. We should probably get this over with."

Lorelei offered a nod of encouragement and they proceeded. Surprisingly, two of the four chairs were already filled. In addition to the lawyer, Sam Travis was also present. Lorelei's eyebrows rose. Then again, maybe she shouldn't be so surprised to see him. He'd obviously cared enough about Wanda to brave her demon cat; it would be like Lorelei's mother to leave him something to remember her by, something of sentimental value. Lorelei studied the tall man, hunched in his chair and staring intently at his folded hands. Sam Travis didn't seem like a man who was easily sentimental.

Ava slid into the chair next to Mr. Stork. That left Lorelei with the seat closest to Sam, a rather pointless distinction since all four chairs were so close their occupants could practically bump knees. With Sam's kindness to her earlier still fresh in mind, she tried exchanging smiles with the man but he wouldn't meet her gaze. The expression froze awkwardly on her face as she took her seat. This wasn't an appropriate time to be grinning at cowboys, anyway. She adopted the air of solemn reserve she used to get through difficult meetings, the ones where she had to tell people things they didn't want to hear, and looked expectantly at the attorney.

Robert's ruddy complexion flushed an ever deeper red as he sorted through pages. "As all three of Wanda Keller's beneficiaries are now present, I shall begin?" In contrast to the words, his tone was pure halting question, as if he were a timid boy asking a parent's permission to stay up past his bed time.

Ava patted his hand. "You're doing fine."

Just how recently had his father retired? Lorelei wondered. He gave the impression this was his first day on the job.

"Thank you, Mrs. Hirsch. We'll start with you, with a message from Wanda." He shuffled his papers some more, stopping a moment later and clearing his throat. "'To my friend Ava, thank you for always being there. I can't express my gratitude for your support over the years. You are such a special, generous soul that even Oberon likes you.'"

Stiffening in her chair, Ava muttered, "The hell he does."

Robert ignored the aside and kept reading. "'I even thought of asking you to be his guardian once I've passed, but ultimately decided that he should stay with the inn. After all, it's his home.'"

Stay with the inn? Lorelei managed not to grimace. How was she going to make that a condition of sale? *Beautiful, well-kept bed-and-breakfast...plus, one evil-tempered feline with possible Satanic affiliations.* Her attention divided, Lorelei listened absently as Robert detailed the personal possessions Wanda had wanted her best friend to have. Among the keepsakes were an antique tea set, a fluted stoneware pie plate, a silver pig charm bracelet and Wanda's dragonfly wind chimes. It was difficult to imagine standing downstairs in the kitchen and not hearing their music tinkling through the window.

Not that she would be standing in the B-and-B kitchen after this trip, she reminded herself. It was right that Ava should take the chimes. They should go to someone who'd known how much Wanda loved them. She'd believed they brought a bit of good luck each time they rang.

Robert turned to Lorelei, his expression apologetic. "You're listed next, Miss Keller.

Do you...need a moment? Before we continue?"

And drag out what had already been one of the longest, most difficult days of her life? "No. Let's keep this moving along," she suggested, her voice tense.

Her tone must have been sharper than intended because Robert flinched. For his sake, she hoped he never saw the inside of a courtroom because opposing counsel would eat him alive. Poor man looked afraid of his own shadow.

"First, there's the matter of your parents' ashes. Wanda Keller asked that her remains and her late husbands' be eventually combined and sprinkled somewhere in the Hill Country, as this was their home. The exact place is to be determined by you, but I can assist you in matters of state law and regulations." He withdrew a thick folder from his briefcase and handed it to Lorelei. "Inside that is a specific itemization and financial statements, but, to summarize, 'I leave my strong, independent daughter, Lorelei, my remaining personal effects, all belongings not specifically tied to the decoration and running of the bed-and-breakfast. I hope she will use my things and remember her mother, who loved her. I also leave her the balance of my checking and savings accounts. To Samuel…'"

Lorelei blinked, confused. She hadn't been aware that Stork had already moved on to the next person. A number of questions churned in her mind. Was the deed to the inn one of the things listed in the hefty folder she'd been given? She tried to process what her mother had meant by "not tied to the bed-and-breakfast." Did that mean the décor in the themed rooms and equipment like the bread machine and coffeemaker were to be sold along with the B and B?

Robert coughed and started again. "'T-to Samuel Travis, I leave all the money in my business account, which he will need to manage the inn as I am leaving him the Haunted Hill Country Bed-and-Breakfast.'"

Chapter Five

Even though Sam had been warned this was a possibility, he could not believe what the lawyer had just said. And he wasn't the only one.

"What?" Lorelei's body tensed, muscles bunched, as if she was going to leap from her seat. Instead she leaned forward, pinning Robert with her gaze. "That can't be right. I think we need a..." She looked blank for second. "A second opinion! I'm dating an attorney back in Philly."

She was? Sam frowned. He couldn't recall Wanda mentioning a boyfriend. Although Sam steered clear of romantic entanglement, if he ever *did* get into a relationship, he'd for damn sure be there for her if she experienced something as devastating as the loss of a parent. Where exactly was Lorelei's legal eagle this weekend?

Sounding more in control of her emotions, Lorelei continued, "I'm sure Rick would be happy to—"

"Are you saying that you want to contest the will?" Robert blanched. "The court doesn't entertain those cases lightly. It requires citing specific grounds that—"

"Why don't we all stop and take a deep breath?" Ava interjected nervously. "Robert, calm down. I don't think Lorelei plans to run out and file a suit. She's just surprised, is all. Give her a minute to adjust."

"That might take more than a 'minute,'" Lorelei muttered. "But thank you, Ava." She was in the process of relaxing back into her chair when she froze, eyes widening. "Ava, you don't seem all that surprised. Did you know about this? That Mom left the B and B to *him?*"

Sam's jaw clenched at her tone. "Excuse me?" He hadn't asked for Wanda to do this! He didn't deserve to be discussed with the same kind of loathing historically reserved for rattlesnakes and horse thieves.

"Well, I'm sorry," Lorelei grumbled, clearly not sorry at all. Her gaze was as sharp as a bowie knife. "But you can't just turn over an established business to someone because you...what? Liked the color of his aura? How did you get her to do this?"

"What do you mean 'get her' to do it?" he growled. As if he were some con artist who looked for opportunities to swindle kind-hearted ladies out of their property?

Lorelei looked momentarily abashed. "I just don't understand. *I'm* her only living family."

Sam saw red. Even though he consciously tried not to dwell on the past, he could still hear his mother's oh-so-sincere tone when she'd dropped him off with his uncle. *Just because I won't be here every day doesn't mean we aren't still family. I'll be back for you, Sammy.* He had no patience for people who were related only when it was convenient.

"Do you think family is just genetics?" he challenged Lorelei. "Because it meant a lot more than that to Wanda. You say you're confused—well, so am I. And what I want to know is, just where the hell have you been for the past two years?"

With that, he got up and stormed out, so ticked off that he temporarily forgot he didn't even *want* the inn.

There was a shocked silence following Sam's departure. No one was more shocked than Lorelei. She kept trying to reconcile the righteously indignant man who'd just given her an earful with the taciturn cowboy she'd first met. *I think I liked him better when he was monosyllabic and uncooperative.*

She turned to Ava and Robert, Sam's parting shot still ringing in her ears. "It hasn't been two whole years," she said. Immediately, she was annoyed both by the sudden need to justify her actions and how lame her attempt had been.

Ava was far too gracious to roll her eyes. "We know, dear. Sam's just..."

"Just what?" Lorelei demanded in frustration. "I don't even understand who he was to Mom."

"Maybe I should give you ladies a chance to talk privately," Robert suggested. Beneath his suit jacket, his shirt clung to him in damp patches. Beads of sweat dotted his forehead, and he eyed the doorway like a hostage evaluating his chance for escape.

Lorelei sighed. "I'm sure you can understand that it's been a difficult day for all of us. Maybe we could talk next week, after I've had a chance to read through this folder you gave me?"

"Yes, ma'am. Absolutely," he said as he stood. "Call me anytime."

"Thank you. There's coffee and lemonade and lots of delicious-looking cakes downstairs. You should try some before you go."

Nodding, he clutched his briefcase close and disappeared down the hall.

Ava shook her head. "Five bucks says he clears the staircase and bolts out the front door in under thirty seconds."

Lorelei chuckled, and the other woman leaned forward to pat her cheek.

"There's the smile that reminds me of your mom," Ava said approvingly.

"I don't look anything like her," Lorelei said, too practical to pretend otherwise, even on a day like today, when she might take comfort in thinking she did.

"Maybe not, but Wanda was all about looking at a person's spirit, not just their face. I'd like to think some of her spirit lives on in you."

Lorelei expelled a puff of air. At least Ava wasn't planning to have tea with her mother's ghost. "You were pretty evasive the other day when I tried to ask you about Sam. Was that because you didn't know how to tell me about Mom's will?"

Ava raised an eyebrow. "The only specific question I remember you asking was if they were romantically involved, which I believe I answered."

"Fair enough. I'll try to be more specific this time. Who is he and why is he here?"

"Sam was working on a nearby ranch during a real dry summer, helping with the horses, and a fire broke out. They got all the animals safely out of the barn, but we hadn't had any rain in months and the fire spread. Once it was put out, he and about half a dozen others needed places to stay. Some of the local hotel owners offered up free rooms, and Sam ended up here. But he wasn't comfortable taking one of the rooms without paying, so he did some work around the inn for your mom. He comes and goes from Fredericksburg, helping with various trail rides and taking different jobs throughout the region.

They got to be close. I think Wanda looked on him like the son she never had."

That hurt enough to knock the breath out of Lorelei. Her mother had left her most valued possession to a man who was "like a son" instead of to the daughter she'd actually had?

Ava tilted her head sympathetically. "Oh, honey. Your mother loved you. She was so proud of you."

"Yeah. I hear that a lot," Lorelei said. What had Sam said when he'd found her sorting through her mother's pictures? That Wanda had looked for opportunities to brag about her?

"I think maybe she worried about Sam. I don't know the details of his childhood, but he doesn't seem to have anybody."

What about all those times after Lorelei's dad had died when *she* had felt alone? She dropped her head into her hands, the irony pounding at her temples.

"You have your life in Philadelphia, a job you love and I'm sure lots of friends there. And apparently a successful lawyer you're dating?"

"Rick," she said numbly. "Rick Caulden."

"What a shame your mother never got to meet him," Ava said.

Lorelei bit her lip, unable to imagine such

an introduction—Rick, in his designer suit and Italian shoes, shaking hands with Wanda, in her tie-dyed tunics and lucky pig earrings. Would Rick have looked on the whimsical older woman with derision? Wanda would have clucked over his long hours and his devotion to the law practice. Lorelei could easily guess what her mother would have to say about his work schedule because Lorelei had heard similar lectures about her own life. *She didn't understand me.*

Which was mutual. Try as she might, Lorelei couldn't understand why her mother had changed her will.

"Are you going to be all right, dear?" Ava asked. "I could get you some coffee."

"No, thank you." Lorelei had put away so much coffee since her arrival that she probably had more caffeine than blood running through her veins. "I think I may go to my room for just a little while." That sounded so much like running away that she added, "To check my work email and voice mail. In case anyone needs me." But she was starting to worry...what if no one did?

Sam met his own reproachful gaze in the rectangular mirror above the old-fashioned dresser in his room. "Not your finest hour, Travis." Provoked or not, it was flat wrong to yell at a lady the day of her mother's funeral. His uncle, were he still alive, would have smacked him upside the head for that outburst in the library.

Although JD Travis had always been forthright about his contempt for his sister-in-law, telling Sam he was better off without a "gold digger who'd dump her own kid," even JD drew the line at being outright rude to a woman. On the few occasions when Rita Travis Hart had remembered she had a son, JD mostly limited his comments to grunts with "ma'am" tacked on the end. He certainly wouldn't have yelled at her, although Sam used to wish his uncle would.

Sam had been poleaxed by the unfairness of life—first losing his workaholic father to a heart attack, then being handed off to an uncle he barely knew so his grieving mother could "get herself together." Her recovery had included finding husband number two—a wealthy businessman from Dallas. Sam had been too afraid of alienating her further to lash out. But he'd dreamed of someone championing his cause and demanding to know how Rita could live with herself, cheerfully creating a second family as if her first one had never existed.

All of which was ancient history and didn't excuse his temper this afternoon.

Sam raised his gaze upward. "Sorry, Wanda." She would have been even less pleased over his behavior than JD. What had she imagined would happen when the news broke? Sam was equal parts touched and exasperated that she had chosen to leave him such a—*burden*—gift.

He went back to that moment when Robert Stork had made the announcement, the look of utter incredulity on Lorelei's face. Any sense of camaraderie they'd shared that morning had been annihilated in an instant. He experienced a twinge of loss almost like a paper cut, sharp and sudden. How much could it really matter if Lorelei Keller disliked him or believed he'd somehow maneuvered himself into her mother's will? He had no doubt Lorelei would be out of Texas as soon as humanly possible, back to her life up north and that Rick guy.

Good. Sam wouldn't be sorry to see her go. In the meantime, however, he wouldn't let her rile him. He decided to go downstairs for a mug of coffee and one of Ava's apricot *kolaches*. If he was able to get a second with Lorelei when she wasn't surrounded by townspeople, he'd tell her he regretted his behavior.

Although some folks were beginning to leave, the crowd was still pretty thick. He nodded to a few people he knew on his way to the kitchen. Ava stood at the sink, drying dishes while Clare Theo washed.

He tapped Clare on the shoulder. "How about I relieve you for a spell, let you get off your feet, darlin'?"

The grey-haired woman smiled up at him. "I'd appreciate that, Sam." She handed him the platter she'd been holding. "I'll be back in a few minutes, okay?"

"Take your time."

Ava glared at him through her glasses. "Well, that was chivalrous."

As opposed to how he'd acted earlier, she meant. "After I'm done here," Sam said, "I thought maybe I'd look for Lorelei. You know where she is?"

"In her room. She mentioned checking in with her office."

On a Saturday? Under these circumstances? The woman was unbelievable. Sam's father had literally worked himself to death, largely ignoring his family in pursuit of the almighty dollar, but even *he* looked like a slacker compared to Lorelei. Sam ground his teeth. Maybe now wasn't the best time to go looking for her after all. It would be difficult to apologize and actually sound sincere.

"You were pretty hard on her earlier," Ava said, in chiding counterpoint to his thoughts.

He'd thought so, too, but maybe they were both wrong. Instead of regretting the times she'd told Wanda she was too busy with her job to visit, Lorelei had simply retreated to her room to work some more. He felt like shaking the woman.

But he hated for Ava to think badly of him. He ducked his head. "Forgive me?"

She pursed her lips in a stern expression, but, behind the spectacles, mischief danced in her eyes. "I can't stay mad at you. Even if I was angry, you've already received punishment enough for one day. After all, *you* are now the proud owner of that cat."

The day had been the longest of Lorelei's life, so why couldn't she sleep? Exhaustion seeped through her bones even as a contradictory restlessness left her tossing and turning. The bed was adequately comfortable, but rest eluded her. Maybe she needed some white noise. The quiet was tomblike after hours of chatter and sniffling and piano music and coffee percolating.

Or maybe she was restless knowing that Sam Travis, self-righteous usurper, was at the far end of the hall, probably sleeping like a baby. Despite their being the only two people under the roof, they'd successfully managed to avoid each other all evening. She hadn't seen him since his dramatic exit from the library. Considering the circumstances, she thought it was rich that *he* was in a snit.

Kicking off the covers, Lorelei gave up all pretense that she might fall asleep soon. *Forget this.* Instead, she decided it was time to try one of the many desserts in the kitchen. She could bring a piece of pie back to her room, maybe grab a book from the library while she was it. She'd already finished the only reading material she'd brought with her, a bound analysis on the mortality impact of medication interruption in post-disaster scenarios. Opening her door as quietly as possible, she crept out into the hall. The automatic nightlights Wanda had always kept plugged in for the guests illuminated the path to the stairs.

She almost missed a step when Oberon shot out of nowhere, zooming up the stairs in some inexplicable feline frenzy. Gripping the banister, Lorelei bit back a string of curse words—maybe her company should consider adding special life insurance policies for cat owners. Her heart was still racing when she reached the bottom of the staircase.

Seeing Sam Travis, shirtless in the arc of light that spilled from the open refrigerator, did nothing to slow her pulse.

What was he doing down here? The knee-jerk question was so dumb she didn't bother voicing it. Obviously he hadn't been able to sleep, either.

He must have heard her coming down the creaky staircase. Without looking back at her, he said, "I'm about to pour a glass of milk and cut into the German chocolate cake. You want a piece?"

Finding herself temporarily mute, she shook her head. At her silence, Sam turned around. Their eyes locked, and she was glad she stood in the shadows. Maybe he couldn't see the blush heating her cheeks. Although she'd been infuriated by the hateful way he'd spoken to her earlier, the anger didn't stop her instinctive female appreciation of his broad shoulders and bare chest. Knowing he'd defined those arms and abs working hard under the Texas sun somehow made them even more appealing than muscles honed through an expensive gym membership. It was a damn shame the man ever wore a shirt. Her gaze slid involuntarily down his body toward the denim waistband of his jeans.

The corner of his mouth kicked up. "You stare any harder, you're going to bore holes into me."

The warmth in her face ignited to full-on flames. She opened her mouth to snap that she hadn't been staring, but the lie stuck in her throat. Instead she advised, "Don't be conceited. Haven't you displayed enough character flaws for one day?"

His expression tightened. "Do you want any or not?"

Cake, she remembered. He'd offered her a slice of the German chocolate. "No, thank you. I'm not much for chocolate."

"One of those women who won't let herself enjoy desserts?" he inquired as he set the gallon of milk on the counter. He let the refrigerator door fall shut, taking most of the light with it. What remained came from a dim lamp above the stove.

"Not at all," she said as she came into the kitchen. "I just don't have a typical sweet tooth. I prefer desserts with extra bite to them. A really tart piece of lemon cake, or something spicy like—"

"Mrs. Hoffman's chili-powder dark chocolate brownies?" His tone was reverent. "Those kick ass."

She laughed. "Agreed." To the dismay of citizens and tourists alike, Bertha Hoffman held the exact recipe a closely guarded secret.

It was surreal to be standing in the dark discussing desserts with this man, when only hours earlier he'd been lambasting her in front of an audience for being a lousy daughter and taking ownership of the inn she'd assumed she would inherit. Would it be easier to talk about the situation now, rather than in a formal setting with an attorney present?

Sam picked up one of the many plastic food containers that lined the countertops and walked toward her in easy, long-legged strides. He moved with a rugged grace that was nearly mesmerizing. "Here." He stopped inches from her. "You might like these. Lemon curd cupcakes, made by one of the women who works at the visitors' center."

"Thanks." She gave him a tentative smile

as she took the container, careful to keep her gaze raised and not ogle his body again. But looking him in the eye was, in some ways, worse. An uncomfortable awareness crackled between them.

He cleared his throat. "Lorelei… I'm sorry about earlier, with the attorney."

Her shoulders sagged as some of the tension she'd been carrying for the last few hours left her body. "Me, too. I know I wasn't very tactful. I was just so caught off guard. She was my *mother,* and she loved this inn." It had hurt far more than Lorelei ever could have predicted to learn that Wanda hadn't left something so important to her only blood relative. It had been like the death of an unvoiced dream, cementing that mother and daughter had never been close enough. And now they never could.

Sam reached out, cupping her cheek with a rough, warm palm. A shiver ran through her body, and he quickly dropped his hand to his side. "If it makes you feel better, I don't know what she was thinking." He turned back to the cake and milk he'd abandoned.

"You said your father died when you were young," Lorelei said softly. "Were you and your mother close?" Maybe it was difficult for him to understand Lorelei's reluctance to visit Fredericksburg because he couldn't relate to how hard each visit had been. Every painfully awkward encounter had been another reminder that Wanda and Lorelei would never have the relationship that was supposed to come naturally to mothers and daughters. Worse, Wanda had never wanted to acknowledge the estrangement. Her cheerfully determined oblivion had only served to make Lorelei feel even *more* isolated.

Sam had tensed the second she asked her question, but he'd yet to answer it. Finally, he spared a glance over his shoulder. "No." He poured a glass of milk and cut a slice of cake without offering any further explanation.

Lorelei sighed inwardly. *The return of Monosyllable Man.* Oh, well. She wasn't sure she could have articulated her and Wanda's relationship, anyway. It was difficult to complain about a parent who had loved you and bragged about you without sounding crazy. Or, worse, whiny. She took a seat at the table and grabbed a napkin, prepared to indulge in a little cupcake therapy.

Directly opposite her, Sam scraped a chair back across the tile. But after a few bites, his fork clattered to the plate.

Lorelei looked up, surprised.

"My mother..." If his words were visible, they'd be the color of rusty water spurting from a faucet too long unused. "I was an only child. Considering the hours my father worked, I'm shocked they even managed to have me. But after he was gone, she sent me to stay with Uncle JD. Said it was just temporary." Sam looked away, but not before she glimpsed the bitterness etching its way into his expression.

"You were there longer than expected." It wasn't a question.

He stabbed at the cake. "'Til I left on the rodeo circuit at eighteen. Don't matter now, of course." His informal speech seemed like a forced attempt at casualness, and he continued without ever looking at her. "But when I was a kid, there would be these days when I was out in the field and I'd see the dust that meant someone was coming down the road and I—"

"You thought it was her," Lorelei added almost desperately. She felt compelled to rescue him from saying the words himself. She ached for the small boy whose hopes had been raised and dashed each time.

He scrubbed a hand over his face. "This

sounds loco to admit, but whenever someone came down that dirt road and it *wasn't* her, I felt like they'd, I don't know, taken something from me. I hope that's not how you felt today, Lorelei. Like I took the inn from you?"

Like you took her *from me.* But it wasn't his fault that Lorelei and her mother had lost their chance to ever be close. A mass of conflicting emotions grew inside her like some malignant tumor.

"I don't even want the inn," Sam admitted with a short, self-deprecating laugh. "What the hell would *I* do with it? Wanda left a legacy of gracious hospitality. She put everyone at ease."

Lorelei's hands clenched in her lap. *Not everyone.*

He took a deep breath. "I can't give you your mother back. But if you want to step into her shoes, run the inn—"

"Run it? I'd be as inept as you!" When he quirked an eyebrow, she backpedaled. "I—I mean, I have a life in Philadelphia."

"Right. How silly of me to forget." He tipped his chair back on two legs, regarding her through narrowed eyes. "I'm sure your Rick is anxious for you to get back."

Rick didn't get *anxious* about anything

but making partner. She waved a dismissive hand. They'd had a mutually beneficial and highly flexible arrangement, not an exclusive relationship. "More importantly, I have a career there. A job I worked hard to get and don't plan to give up so that I can come down here and fix tea and fold guest towels. No, we should sell the B and B. Split the profits," she offered, touched by the way he'd been about to turn over the whole kit and caboodle to her. He'd been important to her mother and, despite Lorelei's shock that afternoon, he deserved to share in the inheritance, too.

His chair hit the floor with a thud and he rose immediately. "Good night, Lorelei." There was no good reason, as far as she knew, for him to have snarled the words.

"Wait." She frowned. "I thought we were talking."

His words carried back to her, muffled. "And now we're not."

Frustrated, she strode after him. She could maybe excuse his storming out of the will reading—after all, he'd apologized for that behavior. But another rude exit in the middle of a conversation? This one actually ticked her off more because she'd thought for a few moments that they'd connected on some level.

"You're going to walk away again?" she demanded from behind him. "Is this a habit with you?"

Since she wasn't prepared for him to stop suddenly in the hallway, she almost lost her balance trying to keep from plowing into him.

"Leaving seemed more polite than staying to speak my mind," he growled as he turned to face her. "You don't want to be in my company right now."

Aggravated past diplomacy, Lorelei rolled her eyes at his soft warning. "Oh, brother. Is that anything like 'you wouldn't like me when I'm angry'? You've already lashed out at me once today, and I survived. Go ahead, cowboy, tell me again what a lousy daughter I was. I'd love to have the stellar insight of someone who barely knows me and never had a single firsthand glance of what my relationship with Wanda was like. Let me have it," she challenged, poking her index finger right below his collarbone. "I can take anything you can dish out."

Chapter Six

She probably *could* handle anything, Sam reasoned. It was probably easy to keep your composure if you had ice water in your veins. He'd foolishly thought he was getting a look at a different Lorelei tonight, one who truly missed her mother and was capable of empathizing with people. She'd even somehow got him to open up about his own family history, which he never did.

So when she'd deftly turned the conversation to "profits" and shrugged off the possibility that there might be actual people in Philadelphia who meant more than her precious career… God. She seemed more like the biological child of *his* parents than a relative of Wanda Keller's.

"Well?" Lorelei taunted.

It seemed criminal that her expression could be so cold after he'd glimpsed a brief flare of unguarded heat earlier. Objectively, Lorelei was attractive—especially with her thick hair tumbling loose over her shoulders, her pink T-shirt and pajama shorts adding a rosy flush to a face scrubbed free of makeup. But the unmistakable desire he'd seen in her dark gaze had transformed her beyond a pretty woman to stunning, an enchantress from a man's dreams. He wanted to make her acknowledge what she'd felt, wanted to do *something* that thawed her the hell out.

Without consciously planning to, he backed her toward the wall. Her breathing grew hectic. Sam tried to ignore the rise and fall of her braless chest just inches from his body.

In contrast to her obvious physical awareness of him, her tone was deliberately bored. "I'm not impressed with the Neanderthal act." Her gaze dropped to his mouth, and Sam hardened.

"It's not an act," he said grimly. The thought of tossing her over his shoulder and dragging her back to his cave was far more appealing than it should have been. When had he leaned in so close to her?

He straightened. "I am going to bed. Alone."

She shoved at his shoulders with both hands. "I sure as hell wasn't volunteering to join you."

"I meant, don't follow me this time," he clarified. But he held her gaze, not stepping aside yet, as he waited for her to agree.

"We'll talk in the morning," she declared.

No, we won't. He turned toward the staircase. He'd already said more than intended to Lorelei Keller, and he didn't plan to make that mistake again.

He didn't bother telling her he'd been hired to help supervise a two-day trail ride out of Bandera. He was packed and planned to get an early start. Sam took the stairs two at a time, confident he'd be able to slip out tomorrow without encountering Lorelei. If he was uncharacteristically lucky, she might even be gone by the time he returned.

When Lorelei woke, sunlight was streaming between the curtain panels. She blinked, her mind groggy and her body tingling. Sudden embarrassment cut through her mental haze and she tried to stifle the memory of erotic dreams flavored with German chocolate kisses. She hurried out of bed, moving with impressive speed for someone with no coffee in her system, and headed for the shower, leaving the water colder than she normally would.

Forty minutes later, she was dressed, her damp hair neatly braided, and feeling in control again. She made her way to the kitchen, telling herself that if she should happen to run in to Sam Travis, he wouldn't make so much as a dent in her equilibrium.

Whether he was wearing a shirt or not. She even walked down the stairs with extra caution, lest Oberon decide it was time to race the Kitty 500 again.

But there seemed to be no sign of man or beast today.

She pulled out the coffee and a filter, then noticed a piece of scratch paper from the notepads Wanda placed in each guest room and by the kitchen phone. Sam's handwriting was an unselfconscious scrawl of black across the pale purple stationery.

L—

I'll be on the road for the next couple of days, so you'll have the place all to

yourself until Tuesday night. If you head back to Philly before then, just lock up when you go. Wouldn't want anything to happen to my inn.
S.T.

She crumpled the paper in her hand. His inn? The man was schizo. Last night, he'd seemed on the verge of giving it to her. Then he'd done a complete about-face, treating her to that obnoxious display of testosterone. Her toes curled at the memory, and she gave herself an impatient shake. She was not the type of woman to go weak in the knees because some bare-chested cowboy leaned over her, looking as if he were about to kiss her senseless and carry her up the stairs.

No, that idea was not attractive at all.

"Rowrrr?" The meowed greeting, more inquisitive than hostile, jolted her from her reverie.

"Morning, Obie." She glanced down. "Hope you weren't looking for Travis. He's gone, and I for one am thrilled. Turns out, he might actually be more of a beast than you."

After an hour of the chuckwagon cook playing harmonica to accompany a "cowboy balladeer," riders were finally turning in for the night, disappearing into their tents in groups of two or three. Armed with a padded bedroll, Sam had opted to sleep outside, where he could periodically check on the horses and the dying fire. It was a beautiful clear night but cool enough that bugs wouldn't be an issue. Away from big cities and towns, the stars were magnificent in the inky sky—almost too crowded for him to make out individual constellations. Why spend the night beneath the colorless canvas of a tent when he could savor this instead?

During Sam's early teens, he and his uncle had often camped in the open air. JD had died years ago while Sam had been working cattle on the other side of the state, but he could still hear the old man's voice in his head on nights like this.

"All you need is right here," his uncle had said. "Texas dirt beneath your feet, a sky full of stars overhead and the occasional Shiner beer—but not 'til you're older, boy. Don't know why my brother could never understand. Instead of appreciating the gifts he had in his life, he worked himself into the ground pursuing the almighty dollar. Your mama's no better, throwing herself at that country club king. But you won't make their mistakes, will you?"

"No, sir," Sam murmured nearly two decades later, his breath creating wispy puffs in the cooling air. The temperature had been dropping since the sun set, and he welcomed the crispness. It helped him think. Now that the riders were bunked down for the night and the peaceful rustling wind had replaced choruses of "Deep in the Heart of Texas" and "Home on the Range," he felt more clear-headed than he had since the morning he'd found Wanda. *I needed this.*

Maybe he'd simply been getting too stir-crazy in the B and B. That might explain his temporary insanity last night. He didn't know which was harder to believe—that he'd almost kissed Lorelei Keller, or that, unless his instincts were *completely* off, she would have let him. They had nothing in common.

Well, they'd both lost fathers at a young age and seemed to have complicated relationships with their mothers. But other than that…

Sam frowned into the blackness. For all that he'd resented his mother dumping him on JD, he had to admit that upbringing had probably saved him. What would he be like now if the Dallas country club king had raised him? Sam couldn't understand why Lorelei had habitually refused her mother's entreaties to come home, why she seemed so disdainful of her roots. Had she ever been lucky enough to see her birthplace the way he did? He folded his arms beneath his head, drinking in the raw beauty of the night.

The only things marring his peace were the unwanted thoughts of Lorelei, buzzing through his mind like mosquitoes. He'd seen real pain in her eyes when she talked about her parents and had glimpsed a wickedly tempting heat in her eyes last night. Was it too late for someone to save the number cruncher from up north? Despite how coldly efficient she could sometimes be, there was real emotion deep down.

Deep, deep down.

Not my problem. Sam put his hands behind his bed and looked up at the thousands of twinkling stars. He had a simple, uncomplicated life that provided everything he needed and it was a shame other people couldn't find fulfillment without their sixty-hour work weeks and cell phones and the ability to check email every ten minutes.

Still, as he drifted to sleep, his imagination provided tantalizing fantasies of what it would be like to show Lorelei the Texas he knew, to see the constant tension around her eyes relax and her mouth curve into a beckoning smile. A sight like that might actually rival the stars.

The storm that rolled in Monday afternoon was severe enough that Lorelei stopped packing boxes to assess the probability of a power outage. She rummaged through several kitchen cabinets and desk drawers in search of candles, matches and flashlights. Rain lashed the windows and the wind outside was howling more angrily than Oberon the summer he'd been sprayed by a skunk and Wanda had given him a bath. But the wind and rain were mere whispers compared to the house-rattling booms of thunder.

Shivering, Lorelei huddled deeper into her sweater. It was one of her rainy day favorites—forest-green ribbed chenille with a zipped-up neckline. She still felt chilled, though, either from the damp weather or the emotional havoc of digging through her mother's memories and trying to parcel them out to various acquaintances and charities. Maybe it was time she took a break from cataloguing and sorting Wanda's personal items and fixed herself a late lunch. It seemed like a good day for soup.

Armed with a flashlight, just in case, she made her way into the kitchen's walk-in pantry. Within minutes, she'd located pasta, broth and canned chicken. Onions hung in a mesh bag over the counter.

"As long as we've got all the basic seasonings and carrots in the fridge, we're in business," she muttered.

The last thing she expected to hear was an answering voice. "Hello?" A man, not Sam or the lawyer, called from the front of the house.

Lorelei was startled enough that she dropped a can on her foot. She sucked in a breath. "J-just a minute." Given the neatly typed sign posted in the front window about the inn not being open for business, she hadn't expected anyone to walk right in without knocking. *Should've locked the front door after walking down to the mailbox this morning.*

She set down her ingredients on the table and limped down the hallway to the entrance. Two men, both dripping water off their coats, stood at the welcome table. They were perusing not the official pamphlets on local attractions, but rather the spiral notebook in which

Wanda had encouraged visitors to write about any "paranormal encounters" they'd experienced in the Hill Country.

"Ooh." The one with the receding hair line waved the little notebook in the air. "Read this part about the nearby Flagstone Guesthouse. It claims that doors open and close by themselves and that things turn on and off for no reason. Lights, faucets, television sets."

Lorelei cleared her throat, announcing her presence. "I'm sorry, but we're not renting out any rooms right now. Or arranging tours."

"Oh, we know." The other man, a shaggy, auburn-haired guy, beamed at her with baffling enthusiasm. "We're not here to check into a room, although that would be awesome. We stopped by because we heard someone *died.*"

"Right here in the hotel," his friend crowed happily.

Lorelei's stomach knotted. These two hadn't been drawn to the inn by stories of Wanda's legendary hospitality and the promise of hot coffee on a cold wet day. They were here because of morbid curiosity, because they were delighted at the idea that someone—*her mother!*—had died under this very roof.

"The woman you're referring to was

Wanda Keller, my mom and the owner," she said stiffly. "Which is why—"

"Has she tried to contact you since she crossed over?" the redhead asked.

His friend groaned. "We've had this conversation, Dwayne. They haven't crossed if they're *still* here."

The bearded fellow, Dwayne, was too excited to debate the point. "Maybe Mrs. Keller could become famous in these parts for haunting the place, like Mrs. Mueller's ghost over at—"

"Show a little respect!" Lorelei snapped. She'd always hated conversations like this, but having to endure her mother's insistence that Lorelei's father wasn't truly gone hadn't been anywhere near as upsetting as these two idiots practically cackling with glee over Wanda's death. It had been less than a week since her death and they were reducing to her to some urban legend. *Where's Oberon when I need him to attack someone?*

The shorter man held up his hands, palms facing her, in a conciliatory gesture. "Your mother based this place on supernatural anecdotes and ghost stories, ma'am. She was interested in the same things we are. I don't think she'd mind our being here."

"I mind." Lorelei was starting to feel slightly crazed. She really should have taken a break to eat earlier. The few instances of spectacular temper in her past had frequently started with an empty stomach and low blood sugar.

"Uh…maybe we should go, Dwayne. We could always check out that Admiral Nimitz Museum over on Main. Some people say they've seen—"

"But we're here already," Dwayne whined. He shot Lorelei a rebuking look. "What could it possibly hurt just to let us look around while we wait out the storm? You don't even have to come with us. Have you experienced any cold spots? Unexplained electrical phenomenon? We just want to compile data on any possible paranormal—"

"Turn you two morons loose unsupervised? I don't think so," Lorelei said. "I want you out of here."

"Morons?" Dwayne gasped. "Now look here—"

"Ghosts don't exist! They're an invention of horror writers and superstitious people who don't know how to let go." *Or how to help their daughters let go.* Lorelei clenched her fists. "I suggest you stop obsessing over the afterlives of total strangers and *get a life* yourselves."

From behind her, a deep voice agreed, "You heard what the lady said. Don't let the door hit you on the way out."

"Sam!" Lorelei whirled around.

He was the last person she'd expected to see today—his note had said he wouldn't be back until Tuesday. His entrance through the back door must have been masked by the ongoing thunder. He looked so sane and solid, standing there in a black long-sleeve shirt and jeans, his customary hat tipped back just enough on his forehead for Dwayne and Dwayne's slightly less moronic friend to get the full impact of his glower.

Dwayne gulped. "When might be a better time to—"

Sam took half a step forward. "Goodbye, gentleman." Perfectly polite words, yet they were laced with enough menace to send the two unwelcome guests scrambling.

Once the men were gone, Lorelei turned back to her unexpected ally. "Thank you." She could have kicked them out herself—had been in the process of doing so—but Sam's presence had certainly expedited the process. What she appreciated the most wasn't even that the men were gone, it was the chance she'd been given to regain her emotions. For a second there, she'd wanted to yell and throw things and she wasn't even sure why. The two men had been a little insensitive, but the chasm between her and her mother had hardly been their fault.

He looked uncomfortable with her gratitude. "Don't mention it."

So what could she safely mention? They'd parted on rather tense terms. Was he disappointed that she was still here? Had he thought about their charged encounter in the hallway the other night? Lord knew she had.

Cheeks heating, she ducked her head. "Have you eaten? I'm about to make soup."

"Sounds good. See you after I change."

With his clothes being so dark, she hadn't immediately realized how wet they were. "Don't cowboys carry umbrellas in their trucks?" Back in Philadelphia, she kept two different size umbrellas in her car, as well as a first-aid kit, emergency cold weather supplies, a spare tire and jumper cables. She'd opted against a flare because of the potential fire hazards and dangerous gases.

He peered at her as if she were speaking a foreign language. "I've helped rescue cattle in flooding situations. I was pretty sure I could get from the truck to the inn without an umbrella."

"Right. Sorry. Carry on." Lorelei's face heated and she marveled at the fact that with one glance he'd made her feel as if perfectly sensible preparations were ridiculous. Or OCD. She couldn't relate to a man whose occupation—not that he seemed to have a steady, constant job—involved activities like riding in rodeos and rounding up cattle in storms. It seemed as if he deliberately sought out risk.

He disappeared up the stairs. Putting thoughts of Sam out of her mind, she studied the spiral notebook that had captivated the two men and sighed. *Speaking of people I can't relate to.* Was it possible Wanda had shared more in common with those men than with her own daughter? Wanda had always seemed more interested in fancy than reality—even though that reality included a scared little girl who needed her.

"What the hell?"

Wondering what had upset Sam, Lorelei hurried up the stairs. His door was ajar and she could see him—hatless, shirtless, but still wearing the damp jeans like a second skin—

standing in the center of the room. "Everything okay?"

He shook his head and pointed, but she had to step farther inside to see what he was indicating.

She looked toward the bed. "Oh, dear." Her eyes widened, and she tried to suppress a laugh. "I guess Oberon wasn't too happy about you abandoning him." The cat had left several…mementos of his displeasure atop the quilted comforter.

"*He's* not happy?" Sam ground his teeth.

"Try to take it as a form of flattery," she suggested sweetly. "He must have really missed you while you were gone."

He picked up a white T-shirt from the back of a chair. She tried not to watch the ripple of muscles in his arms and back as he shrugged into it. "Do you think," he began, his words slightly muffled for a second, "that if we put demon cat in a box and left him on Ava's doorstep she's softhearted enough to keep him?"

"Ha! No way anyone's getting that cat into a box without losing a limb." Not unless they laced his kibble with whiskey and waited for him to pass out.

"You might be surprised." Sam turned

to face her, studying her for a moment with those hypnotic green eyes. His tone took on an uncharacteristic aw-shucks innocence she didn't buy for a second. "After all, I've had a lot of experience with livestock. Gentling the orneriest, feistiest creatures is pretty much my specialty."

While Sam cleaned his bed and carted linens to the laundry room, Lorelei returned to her soup preparations. She diced onions, carrots and celery. *Whack, whack, whack.* The thud of the knife against the cutting board was a bit harder than necessary but cathartic. *Arrogant cowboy.* Unless she was very much mistaken, he'd just lumped her in with his assessment of ornery livestock. *Whack.* If he made so much as one patronizing comment about breaking in fillies, she was going to—

"Smells good," he called as he walked into the kitchen.

She didn't bother answering as she scraped the vegetables into the pot of simmering broth, along with healthy doses of garlic and freshly ground black pepper.

"Impressive." Sam sounded surprised. "When you said soup, I assumed you were opening a can."

Because he didn't think she could cook? "It's only impressive when I have a whole chicken and make the stock myself." Although that took a lot longer, and she was hungry now. She cast a critical eye at the ingredients lined up on the counter. "That's not the pasta I would normally use, either."

He chuckled. "I grew up with a man who had exactly two specialties, only one of which was edible. I'm not picky."

With both of them in the kitchen, the rain outside didn't seem so dreary. It was almost... cozy. But that was an illusion, she reminded herself. After all, they'd been here before—and it hadn't ended well. In her career, she spent a lot of time looking at past trends and trying to minimize risk. She was smart enough to make that work for her in her personal life, too.

"I wasn't expecting you until tomorrow," she said. "Come back early to check on your inn?"

"I was helping with a trail ride. You may have noticed this isn't optimal riding weather." He leaned his elbows on the counter and watched her, his expression inscrutable. "Glad I got back when I did, though. You seemed upset."

"It wasn't a big deal. I shouldn't have let those two guys get to me." She spun away from Sam and his too-close scrutiny and began loading things into the dishwasher, her tone brisk. "That was…uncharacteristic. I normally have control of myself."

"And you think that's a good thing?" Sam asked softly. His tone wasn't argumentative, but it was difficult not to feel defensive.

"Of course I do. I built a career on analyzing facts, then making smart decisions. People need to do more of that and less uninformed reacting. Can you imagine how much better off we'd be if everyone stopped making emotional snap judgments?"

When he said nothing, she looked back at him and was surprised to see him shaking his head and grinning.

Why should she be stung that he didn't agree with her rational perspective? Growing up in this area, she'd always felt like the odd woman out. Sam was just continuing the tradition. "You find my outlook amusing?"

"No, ma'am. I wasn't laughing at you—just the irony. See, I made one of those snap decisions on the drive back. I'd been trying to decide how to tell you about it."

If he needed to tell her, then it obviously

affected her. Despite the words she'd just spoken about not reacting until you had all the pertinent information, nervousness fluttered in stomach. "Wh-what kind of decision?"

"You don't like that your mama left me in the inn," he said. "And, truth is, I don't want it. I have other things in my life that are important to me, and I'm not looking for more. But it feels disrespectful to Wanda simply to hand the place over to you. She could have done that herself and chose not to for reasons of her own."

"Okay," she said slowly. She was following his logic so far; she just wasn't sure where he was leading. "So…?"

"Frederick-Fest kicks off this weekend. I know your mom really wanted you to be here for that."

Something painful twisted inside Lorelei. The last few conversations she'd had with her mother—the last conversations they would ever have—had been Wanda imploring her to come and Lorelei refusing. If Lorelei were the type to subscribe to mystical explanations, she might have questioned whether her mom had somehow had a premonition that this would be their last opportunity to share the town tradition.

"Here's what I propose," Sam began. "You stay for Frederick-Fest, run the booth your mother has already paid for and accompany me and a few tourists on the Haunted Trail Ride next Friday night. And when we get back, I'll sell you the B and B for a dollar."

"Plus there might be legal fees or closing costs for transfer of ownership," she said absently, still trying to wrap her mind around what he'd just offered. "I know the festival was a big deal to Mom, but she never mentioned any trail ride."

He quirked an eyebrow. "Afraid you can't rough it for a night, sleeping on the ground so far from civilization? Might do you some good."

"So this is what, simple pettiness on your part? A hoop I have to jump through before you'll let me have the inn?" *I can handle one lousy camping trip.*

"Is that really what you think? I was serious when I said it might be good for you. Being out there is...a balm to the soul." He said it challengingly, as if expecting her to mock his words. "More importantly, it's a 'haunted' ride—legends shared around the campfire, passing through areas where so-called ghosts roam. The kind of stuff your mother loved."

And I hate.

"Do this for her. You might even have fun."

"I don't understand you. Logically, it makes no sense for you to even give me the inn, much less care whether I stay for the week."

He regarded her solemnly. "Your mother cared."

Lorelei believed that if she met his bizarre conditions, he'd truly give her the place to sell. With the tourism in the area, she was confident she could find a buyer. Even she had to admit there were great attractions nearby. There were all kinds of activities and landmarks for nature enthusiasts; history buffs enjoyed the Pioneer Museum and National Museum on the Pacific War. The Fredericksburg Music Club and the Hill Country Film Festival added touches of culture. Then there was the boom in the regional food and wine industry. On highway 290 alone, leading into town, there were ten wineries, including Lorelei's favorite, Grape Creek. Plus, she'd heard that a major cooking competition was taking place in the area, drawing even more publicity.

Fredericksburg was a great destination. For people who didn't have her memories.

She cocked her head. "And are you planning to stay at the inn for the duration of the festival?"

"That's a problem?" The question seemed to catch him off guard. "We've been sleeping under the same roof so far."

Not for the past two nights. And that last night he'd spent at the inn, when she'd found him in the kitchen… She recalled the glint in his eye, the way he'd leaned toward her in the hall. Her breathing quickened, and she stirred the chicken in with the pasta and vegetables, keeping her gaze locked on the soup.

"No problem at all!" she chirped, mentally kicking herself for even posing the question. For the first time, she wondered about his usual sleeping arrangements. "Where do you stay when you're not here?"

"Variety of places. I have a trailer on some pasture land that's home base. For work in this area, staying with Wanda was always more convenient." He nodded toward the stove. "And the cooking here was always a hell of a lot better."

At that, Lorelei smiled. Her mother had been quite a cook. She'd always encouraged

Lorelei to plan her own birthday menu, telling her no request was too extravagant. On Lorelei's eighth birthday, they'd had a four-course dinner of different kinds of German cookies, followed by a trip to one of the town's amazing chocolatiers. Looking back, Lorelei was stunned she hadn't ended up with a monster stomachache and a mouthful of cavities.

Reliving the memories made her feel strangely exposed, and she was glad when Sam stepped away from her.

He opened a drawer at the end of the counter and pulled out a deck of cards. "You play poker, by any chance? Blackjack? Figure we have a few minutes before the soup's ready."

She wrinkled her nose. "I don't gamble."

He smirked. "Thought as much."

So she was predictable? It was mildly annoying, but she was secure enough not to throw herself into a chair and say "deal me in," just to prove him wrong.

He sat at the table, long legs stretched in front of him, and started laying out the cards for solitaire.

Lorelei couldn't remember the last time she'd seen anyone play the game with actual cards. Usually, it was through a phone app or at the computer while waiting on hold to talk to someone. "You own a cell phone?" she heard herself ask.

"Sure." He flipped over a black ace. "Made a lot more sense for me than a landline. Why, you want the number?"

She shook her head. "I was just…wondering." *Idiot.* What had she thought, that just because Sam was good with horses and wore a cowboy hat he wouldn't know how to text? Fredericksburg might be a historic town, but Sam was not some pioneer frontiersman.

Frankly, she couldn't decide what he was.

He managed to do or say something that surprised her nearly every time they spoke and it irked her that she might be easy for him to peg while he remained a mystery. Her mind was naturally drawn to studying something—*or someone?*—until she fully understood it. Yet caution warned that prolonged observation of Sam Travis could lead to more complications than answers.

Chapter Seven

Sam was too accustomed to waking before sunrise. Wednesday was a rare day off before he spent Thursday and Friday helping set up for the festival. Technically, he could have slept in—yet when his eyes opened at six-thirty in the morning, he knew he might as well start his day.

He could call Grace Torres after breakfast and let her know he had some time free. She'd asked him a couple of weeks ago about a few minor renovations she wanted to make to her family's restaurant, The Twisted Jalapeño. He liked Grace. The young woman didn't fuss and cluck over him like Ava and the other town matrons, nor did she size him up greedily like Barbara Biggins, as if she'd heard that "ride a cowboy" song one too many times. Grace was too preoccupied with her restaurant to have any romantic agendas, which made her easy to be around.

Interesting logic. Because, far as he could tell, Lorelei Keller was about the least romantic woman he'd ever met, but her company certainly wasn't "easy." Corporate priorities aside, she made him uncomfortable in ways he didn't entirely understand or care to examine.

He shook his head and swung his feet to the floor. Lorelei would be gone in less than two weeks. How she made him feel was irrelevant.

It wasn't yet seven when Sam left his room and headed for the kitchen to brew some coffee. But the minute he rounded the corner, the rich, heady scent greeted him and he realized Lorelei had beat him to it. She stood at the counter in a pair of skinny jeans and a cream-colored tank top. Her dark hair was wet, and Sam's body tightened at thought of her in the shower.

He cleared his throat. "You're up early."

She glanced over her shoulder. "Can't seem

to shake the habit, even on days I'm not going into the office. But I actually have a reason this morning. Ava and I are going to caravan to San Antonio and drop off my rental car. Since I'll be staying longer than originally planned," she said pointedly. "I'll just have to bum rides off people for the duration of my stay."

"I can take you to and from the festival next week," he offered.

"Thanks." But from her dry tone, he guessed she was recalling that *he* was the reason she had to go to the festival.

"You've talked to your boss, right?" Did guilt motivate his question? Generally, Sam wasn't one for second-guessing himself, but he couldn't help wondering if his gentle blackmail had been such a good idea.

She nodded. "Yesterday. They approved the additional time and we agreed on some work I could do from here. I'll start compiling data for a trend study and— There you go again," she said, her tone laced with exasperation.

"What are you talking about?"

"Your intimidating scowl," she clarified, sounding not the least intimidated. "You do that when I talk about work. What do you have against actuaries?"

The corner of his mouth kicked up as he admitted, “Darlin’, I’m not even sure what an actuary is.” Although he’d overhead a joke in line at the bank once, that an actuary was an accountant, “but without the personality.”

Instead of sharing that, Sam gestured toward the coffeemaker. “You know a watched pot never brews, right? How about I scramble us some eggs while we’re waiting?” It seemed only fair. She’d made soup for him on Monday; then when he’d got in last night he’d found a note directing him to dinner leftovers that were easily microwaved. Turned out, Lorelei was a damned fair cook.

“I appreciate the offer,” she said, “but I’ll pass on the sit-down breakfast. Ava will be here soon and I still need to fix my hair and get dressed.” She glanced down at her tank top, and Sam couldn’t help following her gaze. Water droplets from her freshly washed hair had made the ivory material translucent in a few places, just enough to tantalize a man’s imagination. “Finish getting dressed, I mean.”

“Yeah.” His voice sounded like a gravel road. *And I have no business going down that road.* “I’ll, uh, pour you a cup to go as soon as its ready.”

"Thanks. I should have been drying my hair instead of standing here. Guess I was hoping I could breathe in caffeinated fumes to help get me going."

She brushed by him, smelling like an exotic flower blooming in the sun—her shampoo or some sort of body wash she'd slathered over her curves? With a hard swallow, Sam realized he no longer needed the coffee to get him going this morning.

Ava beamed at her from the driver's seat and Lorelei bit the inside of her cheek to keep from spouting statistics about how many wrecks resulted from people not keeping their eyes on the road. "I'm just so happy you're staying!"

"For the festival," Lorelei reiterated. *Keep your eyes on the road!* "Not permanently."

Ava pursed her lips. "We'll see. After all, you didn't think you were staying for the festival, either."

Lorelei sighed. "There's a big difference between taking a week off work and uprooting my life. I don't belong here, Ava."

At that, the woman jerked her entire head around to gape. "How can you say that?"

"Ava, would you like me to drive? After

all, you made the trip clear to San'tone for me. Seems only fair for me to drive us back."

"Nonsense. My car can be a little quirky sometimes." She patted the dashboard affectionately. "No one understands her like I do. And stop trying to change the subject, missy. Why would you say you don't belong? This was home your entire life. People love your family in these parts."

They loved Mom. And I'm nothing like her. But Lorelei couldn't say that without crushing Ava, who was childless herself and probably did love Lorelei. The older woman just didn't seem to know she was in the minority.

Lorelei stared out the window, wondering what she would do differently if she had the chance. Come visit her mother, obviously. But that in and of itself wouldn't have been enough to change anything. *What should I have said to her?* Lorelei had tried as an adolescent to explain her feelings to her mother, who'd always offered a vacant smile and assured Lorelei that one day she'd understand.

"Ava, did you ever disagree with Mom?"

"What, you mean like fight with her?" Ava gave a startled frown. "Of course not. Your mother wasn't one for conflict. She was a gentle soul."

Lorelei sighed. *Gentle?* In this case, the apple had fallen so far from the tree, she'd landed in a neighboring orchard. Back in her teen years, she'd been fiercely competitive in her bid for valedictorian. And as recently as Monday, she'd wanted to throttle those two ghost-hunting strangers. Nor did "gentle" describe the way she'd argued with Sam the night before his trail ride. She caught her lower lip between her teeth. She'd been having less-than-gentle thoughts about Sam this morning, too. Not that they'd been arguing.

Maybe it was her morning-brain, often foggy before her first mug of the day, but had there been a moment when the tall cowboy had been undressing her with his eyes? Heat had spiraled through her, leaving her flushed and unsure how to react. One possibility? Pushing him up against the refrigerator and asking him to satisfy her curiosity about his kiss.

"You okay, hon?" Ava's maternal tone was like a well-timed bucket of cold water.

Lorelei couldn't believe she was allowing herself to fantasize about Sam *at all,* much less in Ava's presence. It was like making out in front of your parents.

"Missing your mother?" Ava asked.

The sympathetic question multiplied Lorelei's guilt exponentially. "I, ah, actually wasn't thinking about her just now."

"Oh?" The woman waited a beat. "Come on, tell Aunt Ava. You'll feel better."

"My mind drifted to Sam," Lorelei mumbled. "I barely know the guy but, for all intents and purposes, I'm living with him. The situation is…" Sexually frustrating? "Tense. Sometimes."

Ava cut her gaze toward the passenger seat. "You aren't still mad at him for inheriting the inn, are you? Now that he's giving it to you?"

"I wouldn't say mad, exactly."

"Is this why you asked if I ever fought with your mom? You think she left Sam the place because of some argument you and she had?"

"No, nothing like that."

What Ava said earlier about Wanda veering away from conflict had been entirely true. The closest mother and daughter had come to outright disagreements in over a decade was when Wanda had stubbornly decided that Lorelei needed to come home for this festival, which had been unlike her. And, after hearing Sam's abbreviated tale of his childhood—a veritable orphan with no mother and home to call his own—Lorelei could even understand why Wanda might feel moved to leave him the inn. Lorelei was still shocked that he'd told her about his upbringing, trusting her with something that had to sting even though he said it no longer mattered. She had firsthand experience with how the past could wield power long after you'd moved on with your life.

"I need a drink," Lorelei blurted. She was half joking, rarely the type to indulge. Her favorite self-attributes were a calculator-like mind and control over unruly emotions and baser instincts. Alcohol tended to diminish those.

"Well, we are passing an entire string of vineyards," Ava said.

Oops. Lorelei didn't want "Aunt Ava" to think she'd turned into a lush since moving off to Philadelphia. "I was kidding."

"I wasn't."

"But don't you have sewing to do for the festival?" It had been Ava's idea to start their trip early, so she'd still have the afternoon to work.

"Festival doesn't start until Saturday." Ava lifted one shoulder in a shrug. "I'll get up a couple of hours early tomorrow. Or stay up an extra few tonight. Let's be impractical."

With effort, Lorelei managed not to shudder at the suggestion. Impractical was too close to careless, an invitation to risk.

"We can pull over, try out some local labels and toast your mother's memory," Ava coaxed. "Our version of an old-fashioned Irish wake."

"But you're driving."

"We'll wait until close to town and call Clinton to pick us up—you know there are at least four good places within spitting distance of the inn. What do you say, Lorelei? Your mother always worried you worked too hard and didn't do enough to enjoy yourself. When was the last time you let your hair down?"

Lorelei reflexively fingered her tight French braid. "I suppose a glass or two won't hurt."

Sam enjoyed physical labor. Normally, he could lose himself in the routine of whatever task he completed and wind up pleasantly exhausted from an honest day's work. But today's chores of painting, checking some wiring and changing lightbulbs in hard-to-reach fixtures and repairing rain gutters weren't demanding enough. While his body was busy at the Jalapeño, his mind wandered back to Lorelei. He kept remembering how alluring she'd looked fresh from the shower... although he might have added a few embellishments over the course of the day. He may have pictured even more water spots dotting her tank top before she'd covered it with a gauzy button-down blouse, may have imagined more heated interest in her dark eyes.

He was so focused on Lorelei that Grace had to say his name twice to get his attention, and he jerked himself out of his fantasies with a start—not a smart move for a guy on a ladder.

Grace smiled at him. "I really appreciate everything you've done, but we open for dinner in a couple of hours." During other times of the year, the restaurant was open for lunch as well, but since she was currently busy with the highly publicized cooking contest going on right now, she hadn't been opening until four each afternoon.

He should clean up his tools and get out of the way. "Be right down. This was the last bulb."

She glanced around her and gave a rueful shake of her head. "Considering some of the cracked booth seats and broken tiles that still need replacing, maybe I shouldn't have added more light. Dim makes for better ambience."

He descended onto the floor next to her. "Grace, your enchiladas would be delicious even if guests had to sit in the dark on three-legged chairs." That was the truth, not empty flattery. But no matter how good a cook she was, he knew she was struggling to keep the place open.

He packed up all his stuff and set out a couple of Wet Paint signs, although he'd done the trim work when he first arrived so everything would be mostly dry before patrons began arriving.

"Thank you again," Grace said as she passed him an envelope of cash. He'd quoted the lowest possible price he thought her pride would accept. "I just wish I could afford bigger changes instead of small patch jobs."

"Hang in there," he advised. "Once you win that hotshot competition, you might be able to fix the place up more." He'd overheard enough other people talking about it to realize winning would be a big deal for Grace.

When Sam got back to the bed-and-breakfast, he wondered if Lorelei was inside. Now that her rental car had been returned, there was no way to tell. Not that it mattered. On the nights when she was locked away reading pages of facts and statistics or harassing coworkers by phone, he might as well be alone at the inn. Considering how preoccupied he'd been with her all day, maybc it was best if their paths didn't cross.

He unlocked the back door and stepped inside, resisting an insane urge to call out "Honey, I'm home."

The kitchen was empty, the house quiet.

Sam ignored a brief stab of disappontment and went down the hallway and stopped at the living room, surprised by the sight of two feet hanging over the arm of the couch. One sandal dangled precariously from the wearer's toes; its mate had already lost the battle with gravity.

"Lorelei?"

"Mmm?"

He walked around the piece of furniture and found not only his roommate reclined across the sofa, but also a purring Oberon curled up on her abdomen. Lorelei lazily scratched between the cat's ears. Sam was stunned by the cozy picture they made, but had to admit, if *he* were lying on top of her, he might consider purring, too. He blinked hard, as if he could unsee the mental image now stuck in his head.

She opened one eye, smiled up at Sam, then closed it again. Dark tendrils had slipped loose from her braid, framing her face softly. "Hey. You back from a hard day of riding the range?"

"Actually, I was working closer to oven ranges today. Appears that you two made friends while I was gone." Although Sam and Oberon were back on amicable terms after the cat's bedspread sabotage, Oberon continued to act as if he were doing Sam a huge favor whenever he allowed the human to pet him.

"Turns out, Obie's not so bad after all," Lorelei cooed. "You just have to know how to rub him."

"Uh-huh. So. You look…relaxed." He could have said comatose except for the rhythmic swinging of her foot and the dreamy half smile on her face. There was a day spa one block over; had she gone for a massage?

She arched her back in a full body stretch that made Sam's throat go dry and disturbed the cat, who hopped off the couch with a mew. Her transparent ivory blouse showed off her graceful arms and the swell of her chest beneath the thin tank top. Lorelei sat, frowning as she looked down. "Shoot, now I have cat hair on me." She set her hands just below the collar and ran them down over her body, and Sam forced himself to look away. He should mention that she needed brisker motions to brush off any fur—the slow slide of her fingers wasn't accomplishing anything. Or at least, not what she'd been trying to accomplish.

"Ava took me to a wine-tasting. Several tastings, actually." Lorelei rolled her neck, then leaned back against the couch's headrest. She frowned. "Think we missed lunch, though."

"Ava got you drunk?" he asked disbelievingly.

Lorelei's frown deepened, making her look more like herself and simultaneously making it easier for him to breathe. "Of course not! I do not get drunk. I just feel…" Her pinched expression faded into a slow grin. "Really loose."

Sam could hear his uncle's voice in his head. Before JD went out to dance halls or bars on the weekend, as he applied aftershave and tightened his belt, he'd always pronounced, "Thank the Lord for Lone Star Beer and loose women." It had been his version of "Thank God it's Friday."

"You do not wear expensive suits."

"What?" Sam mentally replayed the last few minutes of conversation, trying to make sure he hadn't tuned out while reminding himself that Lorelei was in no interpretation of the word a loose woman.

Lorelei jabbed a finger at him. "I know a lot of good-looking men who wear expensive suits."

"Like your boyfriend, Rick?" he asked sourly. If she thought clothes made the man, her priorities were more whacked than he'd thought.

"Yes. No. Yes, Rick. No, he's not my boyfriend. But he does look very good in a suit."

"How nice for him," Sam snarled. "If you'll excuse me, I need to grab a shower, so—"

"Some of those businessmen?" She was still pointing her index finger for emphasis. "I think they need the suit to look that good. You don't."

Sam's jaw dropped at the unexpected compliment. He glanced down at the faded T-shirt he wore and the old jeans, now smattered with specks of paint. Then he looked back to her, hit full force by the avid admiration in her gaze. He wanted to express his own appreciation by leaning in to kiss her…except that her mouth was still curled in that crooked, non-Lorelei smile. She might not be flat-out inebriated, but she wasn't entirely herself right now, either. And he needed to get them away from this inn, with its many rooms and many, many beds.

"You know what?" He retreated slowly, as if she were a wild animal that might pounce the moment his back was turned. *I should be so lucky.* "I think you could use some food in your system. And as it happens, I know a great restaurant."

Chapter Eight

After his shower, Sam changed into clothes not decorated with paint smears. When he went back downstairs, he found Lorelei in the kitchen gulping a glass of water.

He couldn't help grinning at her. "You need some aspirin to go with that?"

"No, I'm good." She scowled. "Not that I'm philosophically opposed to taking medicine when it would help me. I just don't happen to need any right now."

He raised an eyebrow at her emphatic tone and bizarre words but didn't pry. "Ever eaten at The Twisted Jalapeño?"

"Nope."

"It may have been called something else before, but I know it's been in the Torres family for years. You like Mexican?"

"Sounds fantastic. I probably should have eaten earlier today," she said sheepishly. "That's the last time I go wine-tasting on an empty stomach."

They walked out to his vehicle together, the gravel crunching under their feet. He opened the passenger door for her and she almost stumbled trying to step up into the truck.

"I'm guessing you're more used to luxury sedans." His words were involuntary and sounded too judgmental to be mistaken for lighthearted ribbing.

She glared over her shoulder. "I'll have you know that my little two-door is completely paid for and I intend to drive it until the wheels fall off."

As he walked around the truck to his own side, he chastised himself. While this might not technically be a date, she deserved some measure of charm—or, at least, not open hostility. He climbed into the truck and flipped the key in the ignition. A rock song blared out of the speakers, making both of them jump. He turned the volume knob as quickly as he could.

"Sorry about that." On the way home, he'd been trying to drown out his own thoughts. Plus, the radio had been playing a song he really liked.

Lorelei rubbed her ear. "Aren't you required by law to listen to country music in your truck?"

He laughed. "I'll make a deal with you. How about we leave our stereotypes here with Oberon and go to dinner—just you and me?"

"I'd like that, Sam. I think I'd like that a lot."

From the outside, The Twisted Jalapeño didn't look like much. There was a simple hand-painted sign, nothing that would light up at night and draw diners from the dark road, and the parking lot was scarred with potholes. Lorelei was undeterred, though. There was a small dive in Philadelphia, nestled among bigger buildings, where she could have happily eaten her own body weight in their cornflake-crusted macaroni and cheese.

Sam opened the door to the restaurant for her, and a hostess with black curly hair brightened at the sight of them. "Back so soon, señor Travis?"

"Working here all day made me crave the

food. Rosie, this is Lorelei. Tonight's her first time at the Jalapeño."

"Nice to meet you," Rosie said with a welcoming smile. "If you'll follow me?" She led them to a minibooth for two. "Your waitress will be out shortly, but I can go ahead and put in a drink order. We have an excellent beer list and daily margarita specials, including our signature chili lime 'rita."

"I'll stick with water and lemon," Lorelei said quickly. She had no intention of imbibing any more alcohol today. Her face warmed as she recalled telling Sam he didn't need a suit to look good. *Probably doesn't need* any *clothes to look good.* The heat blossoming in her cheeks flared even higher and she opened a menu, keeping her gaze lowered. Sam asked for a glass of iced tea and the hostess promised someone would be by momentarily with a basket of chips and the house salsa verde.

The food selections weren't limited to the tacos, nachos and fajitas Lorelei expected. Among the more commonplace favorites she could have found at a dozen other Tex-Mex places were dishes with an unexpected twist to them. Hence the restaurant name, she realized as she scanned the list of entrées. Pork with cucumber-wasabi salsa, curried lamb burritos and spice encrusted chicken with Texas red grapefruits.

Lorelei's curiosity was piqued. "You like fusion food?"

"I have no idea what you just said," Sam said, still studying his menu. "But I like good food, and Grace's recipes are very good."

"She's the one in that contest Ava mentioned?" Lorelei was pretty sure the local chef entered was Grace something.

Sam nodded. "Her grandparents started this place, then her dad ran it for a while, but now it falls on Grace and her two brothers. I'm not sure either of them has been much help lately. One is getting divorced and the other is a police officer. He was injured on the job and is still recovering. In my opinion, this place should be packed every night. Grace has been busting her butt trying to reinvent it."

She couldn't help noticing that he sounded admiring of Grace's work ethic, instead of snarling the way he did whenever Lorelei's career was mentioned. "Well, if the food is as good as you say, I'll definitely be back a few times before I leave town."

A blonde waitress brought them their drinks and took their dinner order. Sam chose the fish tacos and Lorelei went with the chipotle-coffee buffalo steak fajitas.

"You hungry enough for an appetizer?" he asked her.

Lorelei nodded eagerly. All she'd eaten today was breakfast in her car, followed by a small selection of cheeses and some palate-cleansing crackers.

"We'll start with the pot of pork and peppers," he told the waitress.

She beamed at him. "Excellent choice! Personally, that's my favorite thing on the menu."

After the young woman had gone, he explained to Lorelei, "They slow-cook pork with jalapeños and serranos until it's practically mush. Uh, it tastes better than I'm making it sound."

Luckily, that turned out to be true. The spicy pork was incredibly tender and simply fell apart if she tried to stick a fork into it. Instead, she used her spoon to ladle some onto a warm flour tortilla, then nearly moaned at the taste. "Wow." She almost regretted that she had fajitas on the way. "I could happily eat a double order of this and call it a night."

Sam grinned. "I do like a woman with a healthy appetite."

As they ate, he pointed out some of the

things he'd accomplished in the restaurant that day. Discussion naturally turned to her day and they chatted about the afternoon she'd spent with Ava.

"I always think about Ava being friends with Mom," Lorelei said, rolling up another tortilla. "I sometimes forget she and her husband knew my dad really well, too. It was nice to hear anecdotes about him when he was alive and still healthy. I don't know which is worse—losing someone suddenly or having plenty of time to fear the worst and dread it happening."

Of course, her parents had never wanted to talk to her about that possibility. They'd steadfastly insisted everything would be okay as they continued reading books on alternative treatments and miraculous cancer-fighting diets and consulting new age "healers" who were little better than charlatans in Lorelei's mind.

She glanced at Sam. "Did you have any warning that your dad was going to die?"

He gave a harsh chuckle. "My dad was an intimidating man who seemed larger than life, especially to a kid. Maybe he'd been warned by a cardiologist, told to watch his blood pressure or take a damn vacation for once, but none of that trickled down to me. Even if I'd known, I would have assumed he was mean enough to win a fight with the Reaper. He had a coronary at his office and was dead by the time the ambulance got him to the hospital."

"I'm sorry." And not just for Sam's boyhood loss, but for bringing up such a melancholy subject over great food. "I'm a lousy dinner conversationalist, huh? I guess listening to Ava talk about old times got my mind wandering down this path."

Sam seemed to understand her need to revisit the past. "Wanda told me your dad had cancer?"

"The diagnosis was grim from the beginning." They'd never admitted that to her face, but she'd strained to hear the whispers on the other side of closed doors. "My father refused the radiation and chemo, which he called poison. He'd read just enough 'spontaneous recovery' stories to believe something like that could happen to him. Mom kept chirping about the power of positive thinking, like all we had to do was *want* him to get better enough and he would. You've seen the Peanuts Halloween special where Linus waits in vain all night for the magical pumpkin to come, then vows to try harder the next year? I felt like that, like I just hadn't hoped sincerely enough. Dumb, isn't it?" Her mouth twisted in a bitter, self-deprecating smile, inviting him to laugh along at her childish folly.

But Sam's expression was somber. "Lorelei—"

"Here you go!" The waitress's voice seemed too loud and too perky. But the food she carried smelled wonderful, reigniting Lorelei's flagging appetite. After the woman had admonished them to be careful of the hot plates and gone on to her next table, Sam tried again to voice whatever he'd been about to say.

But Lorelei cut him off with an emphatic shake of her head. "You know what? This all looks fantastic, and I think we should dig in."

He watched her for a moment, and she thought he might speak his mind anyway. Lord knew he wasn't shy about doing so. But then he asked, "You want to try a bite of my tacos?"

"Yes. Thank you." Both entrées were delicious and she strove to enjoy them, putting aside her bleak reminiscing.

"So I've traveled all over the state," Sam began, "and know a lot about regional cuisine here in Texas. But I've never been up north. What's good in Philadelphia?"

She was grateful for the chance to talk about her adopted home, the place where she'd shucked her past and became the person she was meant to be. "I guess a cheesesteak sandwich is the most obvious. A lot of lifelong residents love turtle soup, but I haven't been able to acquire the taste." She told him about her favorite Stromboli vendor near her office and how much she loved holding a warm soft pretzel on a cold day. "And there are *many* cold days." The mornings when she had to shovel snow were the times she felt most nostalgic for Texas.

"They sell giant pretzels at the festival," he reminded her. "I'll have to get you one."

She flashed him a wry smile. "You're giving me the inn in exchange for staying. I don't need the added incentive of a pretzel."

"Y'all doing okay over here?" The bouncy waitress had returned. She refreshed their drinks, smiling extra brightly at Sam before departing again.

Lorelei laughed. "I think our server has the hots for you."

He blinked, looking startled by the observation. "What? Why would you say that?"

"For starters?" She dragged a napkin around her glass. "There's this puddle of water because she couldn't take her eyes off you long enough to pour." Lorelei watched him fidget in his chair. *Don't tell me the big, strong cowboy is embarrassed!* "Oh, come on, Travis. You can't be that oblivious. Women probably ogle you all the time. You're…"

He raised his head sharply. "Yes?"

She shrugged. "You know…*you.*"

A slow, purely masculine grin lit his face, making his expression one of the sexiest she'd ever seen. "Uh-huh. Well, that certainly settled the matter."

She fought the urge to throw her soggy napkin at him. "Stop fishing for compliments. It's unbecoming."

"Not fishing," he protested. "I've already hit my quota of compliments for the day. What with your remark about how good I look even without a suit—"

She groaned. "It's not very gentlemanly to bring that up." Mellowed by the fading remains of her wine buzz, she had been far too open with her thoughts. If Sam hadn't left so soon to take a shower and change, would she have wound up confessing how often she'd thought about him kissing her? "I was hoping you'd forgotten."

"Forget an admission from you? You are many things, darlin', but forgettable is not one of them."

She was afraid to ask what the "many things" entailed. There was a good chance they wouldn't all be flattering. Conversely, anything too flattering could boost the simmering awareness between them. She was relieved they'd gone out for dinner tonight, somewhere safely public. The rest of her stay should be easier to manage with the festival to keep them busy.

"So, friendly waitresses aside, you have any ongoing romantic relationships?" Surely if there were someone serious in his life, he—or Ava—would have mentioned it by now. Lorelei certainly hadn't crossed paths with any women coming from the direction of Sam's bedroom.

"Not really. I travel a lot, keep an erratic schedule. I have lady friends in different towns who I'll maybe call for dinner if I'm coming through."

Dinner followed by breakfast? When he wanted to be, Sam was charming. It wouldn't be difficult for him to rack up a "lady friend" for every zip code he visited. Then again, he didn't really give off the vibe of a player. He was unabashedly plainspoken, not the type to string women along with slick phrases or insincere promises.

"I'm not looking for anything lasting right now." He made a face and added a muttered, "Although some women can't seem to get that through their heads."

He seemed too irritated for it to be a general comment. "You have a specific stalker?"

"As a matter of fact. But it seems impolite to tell you who." He affected a look of comical fear. "Besides, I'm pretty sure if we accidentally say her name three times, she materializes."

Lorelei laughed. "Well, we wouldn't want that."

"Sam!" A tiny, dark-haired bundle of energy in a bright red chef's jacket hurried to their table—obviously not an unwanted stalker, since he looked delighted to see her.

"Grace, dinner was wonderful, as usual. And you've made a new convert tonight." He swept a hand in Lorelei's direction. "Grace Torres, meet Lorelei Keller."

The chef's pretty features puckered in a frown. "Wanda Keller's daughter? I'm so very sorry for your loss. She was a lovely woman. She often visited my aunt in the nursing home and listened to her spin tales, like the time *Tía* Maria swears she encountered *La Llorona.*"

At Lorelei's blank look, Sam explained, "The weeping woman, a figure in Hispanic folklore."

Grace nodded. "*Mi tía* looked forward to those afternoons. Your mother will be greatly missed. Dinner is on the house for you two!"

After what Sam had told her about the restaurant's struggles, Lorelei was touched by the offer but loath to accept. "Oh, let us pay! Please."

"Out of the question. Your money is no good here." Grace winked. "At least, not tonight. But you'll come again soon, yes?"

"Definitely," Lorelei agreed. "I was already planning to return while I'm in town."

"Will you be here long?"

"Only through the festival. But I may have to come back once or twice before the inn's final sale."

"You're not keeping it?" Grace asked, sounding surprised. "Taking over the family business?"

Lorelei recalled what Sam had said about

this restaurant, how it had been passed down through three generations. "Mom didn't buy the inn until after I'd moved away for college. I don't really see it as the family business."

"Understandable," Grace said after a moment. "Well, good luck finding new owners. You two enjoy the rest of your meal."

At the back of her mind, Lorelei kept thinking about potential future owners. What kind of people might her mother want in charge of the inn—another empty-nester like Wanda herself, supernatural enthusiasts like the two who had barged in earlier this week? It wasn't until after they'd left the restaurant that Lorelei asked Sam, "When Mom left you the inn, do you think she really believed you'd keep it?"

Sam was quiet, and it was too dark in the cab of the truck to read his expression. "Hard to say what your mom thought. She...had her own way of viewing the world."

"That's the diplomatic way of putting it," Lorelei mumbled. Her peers in school had been less tactful about their opinions of her "kooky mom."

"I didn't mean it as an insult," Sam clarified. "My father and mother and stepfather all bought in to the same skewed keeping-up-with-the-Joneses values that thousands of other people share. I always liked that she was unique." A beat later, he added, "Of course, I didn't grow up with her."

It seemed like a big concession, his finally admitting that there might be more than just Wanda's side of the story, and the sympathetic note in his tone warmed her to the core. She stole a glance at his profile, thrown into relief by a streetlight, and repressed a sigh. In the week she'd known Sam, he'd demonstrated loyalty, humor and dependability—*and* he had the face of a rugged angel. Add in an ability to admit when he was wrong and it suddenly seemed a shame that he didn't want a girlfriend in his footloose life. Some woman might have been lucky to have him.

As they reached the back door of the inn, they simultaneously went to unlock it.

Lorelei drew up short to avoid a collision, and Sam stepped out of her way, moving to the side of the tiny concrete slab that didn't quite rate back-porch status. "You go ahead," he said. "It was just habit." In addition to each of their sets of keys, Ava had one, too.

She unlocked the door and preceded him into the kitchen, suddenly feeling awkward. If this had been a date, this would be the part of the evening where they kissed good-night. *Assuming we stopped with a kiss.*

Sam leaned against the counter, glancing at his watch. "It's still pretty early. Would I bother you if I watch television for a while?"

The individual rooms didn't have TVs, but there was a big screen in the living room. Lorelei knew her mother had often used the DVD player to do movie nights for the guests—not just films that suited the supernatural theme of the inn, but also holiday classics during appropriate seasons and romantic favorites when she had a houseful of couples.

"You're welcome to join me," he added belatedly. His tone seemed skeptical, though, as if he were trying to imagine what might appeal to both of them equally.

"You go ahead," she told him. "I plan to fire up my computer and work on the trend study." That was how she would have spent her afternoon if she hadn't come back lethargic from the wine. "'Night, Sam. Thanks for dinner."

Straightening suddenly, he stalled her with a hand on her arm. "Lorelei, wait."

His unexpected touch was warm through

the insubstantial material of her blouse. Her mouth felt dry, and she licked her lips. "Yes?"

His hand slid off of her, and he shoved it through his tawny hair as he gathered his thoughts. "About your work." He flashed a teasing grin. "About my scowl?"

She grinned back at him, helpless not to in the face of those dimples. "What about it?"

"I said at the memorial service that most of my recollections of my father are hazy. But not all of them." He stopped, as if sharing this kind of thing didn't come naturally to him, then huffed out a breath. "You told me a bit about your dad over dinner. I should be able to return the favor. Especially since it indirectly affected you."

She raised her eyebrows, curious to hear what he had to say but sensing he might withdraw if she pushed.

"There's one very clear memory. I'd confronted him about breaking promises. He hadn't come to a baseball game, missed my hitting a home run or something. Seemed important at the time."

Looking at the powerful, broad-shouldered man in front of her, Lorelei couldn't quite picture him as a little boy. But even with the gruffness of his tone, she could hear an echo of that boy's crestfallen disappointment.

He shook his head. "I don't really remember the game. But I recall vividly the contempt on his face. He told me to man up, quit whining. Said I needed to understand his job was more important than a bunch of kids stumbling through nine innings and that when I got older, when I had a family to support, I'd be just like him."

"Clearly not father-of-the-year material," Lorelei murmured. Was this one of the reasons Sam chose not to commit to a single steady job or work nine to five in an office somewhere, because he couldn't stomach the thought of fulfilling his father's prediction?

"In answer to your question this morning, I don't have anything against actuaries," Sam said ruefully. "Just a chip on my shoulder about people who seem married to their jobs. Which is no excuse for being a jackass to you."

It might not have been the most eloquent apology ever, but it had been incredibly personal. She didn't know how to respond. Part of her wanted to hug him, which startled her. Lorelei was so not a hugger. If she had been a gambling woman, she would have bet the farm Sam wasn't, either.

His lips quirked in a sardonic smile that never fully materialized. "Guess we both have some lingering anger toward our dads to work through."

She blinked, trying to make the transition from the unanticipated tenderness she'd been feeling to his bizarre assessment. She had memories of her father telling her long bedtime stories and tickling her until she shrieked—he'd been nothing like the cold businessman who made a child feel worthless. "I'm not angry with mine."

Rocking back on his heels, Sam shot her an incredulous look. "I was with you at dinner, remember? It's okay to be bitter about what happened."

"A good man got sick and died too young." She kept her voice level as she recounted the facts. It had been so long ago; bursting into tears now wouldn't change a damn thing. "I suppose I am bitter about the unfairness of the situation. But I'm not mad at *him*. My dad loved me."

"Just not enough to seek medical attention?" Sam asked softly.

Her entire body jerked. "How dare you? That's a horrible—"

"I'm not suggesting it's true," he said with exaggerated patience. "Just acknowledging how a daughter could feel that way."

Lorelei dug her fingernails into her palm. She'd agreed to stay for the festival—letting the world's least likely shrink psychoanalyze her in the meantime hadn't been part of the deal. Didn't he know she was having a difficult enough time with losing her mom this week? To drag up the past and relive losing her father on top of it…

She tried to numb the grief that threatened, her tone cool. "Even with treatment, there was no guarantee he would have made it. Second-guessing his decisions two decades after the fact would be completely irrational."

For some reason, her words seemed to rankle him. "I'm talking about emotions, not quantitative algebra."

"Like you know so much about quantitative algebra?" she snapped. What she really meant was, *Like you know so much about me?*

His body went still as his eyes narrowed. "Right. Because you're the Ivy League grad and I'm the dumb hick cowboy?"

"That's not—"

He took a step back, in the direction of the door behind him. "Changed my mind 'bout that TV. Think I'll shoot some pool in town. Don't wait up."

Lorelei gnashed her teeth as he disappeared into the dark. The man might claim his specialty was taming ornery livestock, but as far as she could tell, his true expertise was in abrupt exits. She revised her earlier opinion about his dating life. Thank heavens he *wasn't* interested in a relationship. Any woman foolish enough to fall for Sam Travis would develop shin splints and bad knees from constantly having to run after him.

Since the two pool tables in the small bar were both in use and Sam had no interest in drinking, he ended up at the dartboard, playing Oh-One with a stranger who'd introduced himself as Ty. Sam wasn't sure whether Ty was a local, hired help for the festival or a tourist just passing through—the dark-haired man showed as little inclination toward small talk as Sam.

I've learned my lesson. Sam threw the first dart of his turn. He'd done too much yapping for the night already and planned to keep his trap shut going forward. Whatever uncharacteristic impulse had motivated him to share another piece of his past with Lorelei…well, that urge was long gone now. He was surprised he'd given in to it in the first place.

Wanda had always tried to coax him into "bonding" with other people. "Or at least smile more," she'd say. "If you're not careful, Sam, you're gonna scare away all my other guests."

Tonight was the second time he'd let himself get suckered into a false sense of connection with Lorelei, only to have his misreading of the situation turn around to bite him on the ass. He'd seen the pain in her face over dinner as she talked about her father's death, the guilt and hurt that she'd never been able to join in her parents' optimism. Even though he thought she'd been blessed to have Wanda as a mom, Sam did know what it was like to feel outside your own family. He'd always fallen a distant second in his parents' priorities. While Sam hadn't enjoyed talking about his father, he'd stammered through it. For a heartbeat of time, he'd felt he and Lorelei had found a patch of common ground.

Then the pity in her eyes—already galling—turned to annoyance and she haughtily informed him that *her father* had loved *her.* Then she'd become condescending and he'd had to leave before he lost his temper. It was ironic, really. He'd briefly dated a woman or two who'd tried their best to get him to open up, but he'd never been tempted to do so. Until Lorelei, who wasn't interested.

Won't happen again. Hell, he'd give in and date Barbara Biggins—a blue-eyed piranha in a miniskirt—before he made himself vulnerable to Lorelei again. He flung his third dart, and it went wide, bouncing off the rim of the board before falling to the ground. A growling noise sounded low in his throat, and Ty raised his eyebrows but said nothing as he walked to the throw line.

Several more rounds passed as each of them, lost in his own musings, whittled his score down to zero. Despite a few lucky throws along the way, Sam couldn't find the precision to hit the exact numbers needed. *Could be worse.* At least they weren't playing for money. He heard Lorelei's disapproving tone in his head as she'd informed him, "I don't gamble."

Of course she didn't. She also didn't relax, didn't visit her only family when she'd still had the chance, didn't let herself feel.

But even as he mentally listed those faults,

he knew they weren't true. Not entirely. If she were as cold as she sometimes appeared, she never would have gotten under his skin like this. It was those moments when the veneer cracked and he witnessed the emotion beneath…

"I'm gonna go out on a limb here." Ty broke the silence, his tone more resigned than curious. "Woman troubles?"

Sam dipped his head in a curt nod.

"Know the feeling." Ty tossed a dart and missed by a mile. "Good luck."

He didn't need luck. He needed Lorelei to sell the inn and go back where she belonged. But, somehow, looking forward to that didn't give him quite as much peace of mind as it should.

"Oh, Ava." Lorelei tossed the pamphlet she was supposed to be folding onto Ava's dining room table. Her creases were completely crooked, the tri-fold uneven. "I'm a bad person."

Coming into the room with a pitcher of lemonade, Ava paused in the doorway. "Is this about drinking wine in the middle of the day again? Because those tasting sizes are tiny. It's not like you had twelve actual glasses."

"I wasn't talking about wine." Lorelei would have laughed if she weren't plagued by the look she'd glimpsed in Sam's eyes last night.

After he'd first stomped out of the inn, it had been easy to hold on to her anger. But as she'd tried to settle into her work, she kept recalling that split second just before he'd announced he was going into town. When his green eyes had flashed with insecurity. *That I caused.* Until this trip, she'd firmly believed that the reason she didn't have a serious—and therefore time-consuming—romantic relationship was because she wasn't looking for one. Could it possibly be because she didn't deserve one?

Ava set the lemonade down next to the glasses she'd already placed on the side table. "So what heinous crime did you commit?"

Lorelei bit her lip. She knew Ava cared about Sam, even though she didn't know him as well as Wanda had, and Lorelei hated to admit that she'd insulted him. "Well, after you and Clinton dropped me off yest—"

The doorbell pealed, and Ava held up her

finger. "Hold that thought, dear. Those must be the girls."

Lorelei heard female voices at the front door and greetings being exchanged. Then Ava returned with four other women. Ava's definition of *girls* applied to multiple generations. Gertrude Hirsch, Ava's mother-in-law, was in her mid-seventies. There were two middle-aged women, both of whom Lorelei recognized from the memorial service although she couldn't recall their names, followed by a round-faced redhead who probably still got carded when she bought a beer.

As soon as Ava had helped her mother-in-law into a chair, she pointed to the redhead. "Lorelei, you remember Tess Fitzpatrick? I believe the two of you were in the same graduating class."

Tess smiled brightly, her brown eyes warm. "Lorelei is the reason I passed geometry!"

"I was?" She was embarrassed not to remember, but then, Lorelei had spent most of her teen years preoccupied with getting away, counting down the days and weeks until college.

The redhead nodded. "Mrs. Sumner asked you to tutor me when I was in jeopardy of failing. You were a hard taskmaster, but you certainly got me straightened out!"

At the behest of the math department, Lorelei had tutored multiple students during her four years in high school, and she suspected "hard taskmaster" was among the nicer things they'd said about her. She frowned inwardly, chiding herself for the knee-jerk negativity. Maybe there were others who, if not as instantly friendly as Tess, bore her no ill will. Not all of her former classmates had been as spiteful as Babs Biggins and her clique of friends, quick to label Lorelei a misfit math nerd and laugh about her zany mother.

"So should we work first and take a break for refreshments later," Ava asked, "or start with the snacks? I made a fresh batch of peach-pecan cornbread this morning."

The women were all here to help with various projects for the festival. Gertrude had originally founded a dance school in town called "The Hirsch Hoofers." It had undergone a name change and several shifts in management and Tess now worked there, teaching little girls tap and ballet. Ava and Tess had some last-minute sewing to do on costumes, as several of the classes would be performing this weekend.

"Lorelei came over with her brochures printed and needs some help folding them," Ava said. "She also needs some suggestions for decorating. No offense, dear, but you don't quite have your mother's imagination."

Lorelei couldn't help but chuckle at the colossal understatement. "Don't you think I should keep it low-key, though? After all, I'm not really trying to promote the inn. We're not even accepting reservations right now. I just want to do this as a goodbye to Mom." Maybe she'd first agreed to man the booth because it was an expedient way to get the inn, but attending the festival felt right. Even before Wanda had become a local business owner with her own booth, she'd always attended. Lorelei couldn't remember a year her mother wasn't there. *This'll be the first.*

Tears burned the back of her eyes as she pictured Wanda, her clothes smeared with powdered sugar from a warm funnel cake. Or Wanda cajoling her daughter to try on silly souvenir hats with her.

"Lorelei, dear?" Ava's voice was gentle. "Why don't you help me in the kitchen? Ladies, glasses are right there. Help yourselves to some lemonade."

"Thank you," Lorelei said once they were

alone in the kitchen. She took a deep breath to regain her composure. "I appreciate the excuse to get away from an audience."

"Certainly." Ava reached up into a cabinet to pull out small dessert plates. She set them on the counter then stood there for a moment as if weighing her words. "But Lorelei? You know that no one in that room would think less of you for missing your mama or showing your emotions. Feelings aren't weaknesses."

"You sound like Sam." At Ava's questioning glance, Lorelei added, "He gave me similar advice last night." He may have been a bit more sarcastic about it once goaded, but the sentiment boiled down to the same thing.

"Then, he's a smart man."

Lorelei flinched, recalling his dead tone. *I'm the dumb hick cowboy.* That wasn't remotely how she saw him. She found him exasperating, even infuriating on occasion, but not unintelligent. If anything, he discomfited her sometimes because he seemed too perceptive.

Suddenly, she was eager to get through the festival preparations with the other women. As soon as they were finished, she had a cowboy to find.

Chapter Nine

The wind whipped fiercely around Sam and the other workers dotting the Marktplatz, a landscaped public area that was home to the historic Vereins Kirche and considered by many to be the heart of town. Although there was already a permanent pavilion, along with many picnic tables, other tents and temporary stages needed to be erected. Tomorrow, sound systems would be wired and checked. The festival would host performances that ranged from dog-training demonstrations to four-year-old ballerinas to the live music of Praha Polka Party.

Sam was currently hammering in stakes

along with Andy Schubert, one of the coaches at the middle school who'd come to help after classes were done for the day.

Andy eyed the sky, overcast with ominous clouds. Weathermen had been predicting another big storm. "Hope this holds off until we're finished up here."

"Holds off 'til tonight and blows over before this weekend," Sam added. He didn't think bad weather would kill attendance completely, but it could certainly make the festival muddier and less cheerful.

Andy grunted in agreement. "I'm guessing the Battlin' Billies Marching Band and everyone who's been building parade floats—Whoa. Who is she and why don't I know her?"

Sam wiped a hand on his jeans and looked up to follow Andy's gaze. *Lorelei?* He frowned, surprised to see her striding toward them across the lawn. Her long hair was loose today, swirling around her face and shoulders with each gust of wind. She had on a pale pink sundress with another one of those see-through blouses—this one the color of strawberries, with shiny collar and cuffs—buttoned over it. Her skirt kept flaring out around her calves and twisting between her legs. He found himself staring as if mesmerized by the motion. Or maybe just by her shapely legs.

Sam jerked his gaze away from her and back to Andy, who wasn't nearly as much fun to look at. "That's, ah, Lorelei. Keller. Wanda's daughter."

"Think she has any interest in being the future Mrs. Andy Schubert?"

"She's seeing a guy back in Philadelphia, where she lives." And if Lorelei had already explained that she and that attorney guy only dated casually…well, Andy didn't need to know all the nitty-gritty details of her life.

"Bummer," Andy said.

Sam stood. "I should go make sure everything's okay. Be right back." He walked off without waiting for an answer, wondering what was important enough for Lorelei to track him down. Had something happened at the inn?

She stopped, trying unsuccessfully to keep her hair from tangling about her face, and offered him a tremulous smile. "H-hi. I took you away from what you were working on."

"They won't fire me if I take a five-minute break. What's up?"

"I…" She broke their locked gazes, staring

intently at the ground. "For the record, you made this look a lot easier last night."

He stiffened at the mention of the previous night, recalling his resolution at the bar to keep his distance from her. "Made what look easy?"

"Apologizing." She raised her eyes then, genuine regret clear in their coffee-rich depths. "Sam, I'm sorry about how I spoke to you. How I might have made you feel."

He was shocked by this overture but experience with Lorelei had taught him not to let his guard down. "Don't mention it. It's forgotten."

She reached out to clutch his arm, as if she was afraid he'd walk away from her. "Will you be done here soon? I'd like to buy you a drink. Or maybe something from one of the chocolatiers?" She swiped a thumb across her cheek. "I think that was a raindrop."

Had the rain begun already? All he felt was her grip on him. "You should get back to the inn, stay dry."

"Uh… I actually had a friend of Ava's drop me off on Main Street on the way to one of her errands. I was kind of hoping to get a ride back with you." She bit her lip. "No car, remember?"

He sighed, realizing he wasn't going to be able to shake her loose. "Wait over under the pavilion. I should be finished up soon."

"Anything I can do to help?" she asked, her voice tentative and very un-Lorelei.

He wanted to squeeze his eyes shut and block out the earnestness in her gaze. Just as he'd acknowledged last night, it was these chinks in her normal armor that got to him. "Thanks, but Andy and I have it covered." If the skies truly opened up in the next few minutes and the scattered drops became a torrent, the flimsy material of Lorelei's blouse and thin cotton dress would be plastered to her body. "*Please* stay here."

She nodded. "Whatever you say, Sam."

He'd seen Lorelei coldly remote before and spitting mad, but like this—cheerfully accommodating and eager to please? This, he realized, was the woman at her most dangerous. *I am so screwed.*

At first, Lorelei had thought Sam would refuse her offer to buy him dinner or a drink. Yet once they were buckled into his truck, he'd relented. She breathed a little easier as he steered them toward a place where Sam said the barbecue was decent. Lorelei was an extremely independent person who was uncomfortable feeling beholden to other people—even sharing her workload with Celia had driven her a little nuts. After all Sam had done, from offering to give her the inn to his willingness to listen to her talk about her family, she desperately wanted to repay his kindness.

She hadn't meant to become bitchy and defensive last night when he'd brought up their fathers. His insight had simply thrown her. It sounded disloyal and illogical for a daughter to be mad at her father for contracting a disease he'd had no control over.

Somewhere between the Marktplatz and their destination south of town, the steady drizzle began pelting them with real force. Sam increased the speed of the windshield wipers twice before they pulled into a mostly empty parking lot. She guessed that the tables on the covered patio were a popular place to eat when the rain wasn't coming down in billowing sheets.

Sam's sudden laugh took her by surprise and she whipped her head around to find out what was funny. He gave her a sardonic smile. "I guess this evening would be the perfect time for one of those 'umbrella' devices

I've heard tell of. Here." He leaned toward the steering wheel, shrugging out of his denim jacket. "It's not exactly waterproof, but it'll help."

She wanted to tell him that the gesture was sweet but unnecessary. Except that her words evaporated as she studied the muscles in his arms. It was ridiculous how good the man looked in a short-sleeved black T-shirt. The denim was still warm from his body, and when she shrugged into it, Sam's scent enveloped her. It was as though he'd let her borrow an embrace rather than just a coat.

He reached for his door handle and flashed her a rakish grin. "Ready to make a run for it?"

Laughing, they bolted through the rain. By the time they reached the entrance, Lorelei's hair clung to her face in wet ropes and she knew what little makeup she'd applied that morning was probably streaked unattractively across her face. But she couldn't bring herself to care. In fact, she felt breathlessly giddy in a way she hadn't since she was a young girl.

Inside, the country music twanging through the sound system competed with the rolling thunder and the rain splatting against the metal roof. This was a multipurpose place, serving as bar, restaurant and dance hall. There wasn't much of a crowd, but a few couples swayed on the red oak floor.

"You mind sitting at the bar?" Sam asked. "The food's good, but most of the tables are out on the patio."

"Bar works for me."

They found seats and consulted the menu, which was nothing like the complex offerings at Grace's restaurant. No, here the food choices were simple and limited: pork barbecue sandwich, pork barbecue ribs, coleslaw, baked beans, side salad and steak fries. Period.

Lorelei chuckled. "What, no dessert menu?"

Sam pointed toward the fully stocked bar opposite them. "I think they make some kind of chocolate martini thing on request. But you'd probably be more of a lemon drop girl. I know how you like a little tart with the sweet."

A ruddy-faced bartender with freckles peeking out around his dark red beard came over to them and greeted Sam by name. Then he took their orders of two sandwiches and a side of fries to split. By the time the food came out, people had started trickling into the bar.

Sam checked his watch. "Must be about time for happy hour."

Lorelei swiped one of the thick fries through ketchup and popped it into her mouth. She closed her eyes in bliss. "If I lived in Fredericksburg, I'd be here every night for the fries alone." When she opened her eyes again, she shook her head. "That settles it. I can't ever move back. Between Grace's restaurant and these fries and the chocolate shops on Main Street—"

"And the vendors at Oktoberfest and sausage from Dutchman's Market," Sam added.

"Exactly. I'd be the size of a house." She grabbed another fry. "But since I'm leaving soon, might as well enjoy it while I'm here!"

Sam leaned back on his bar stool, his expression pensive. "Do you ever think about coming back? Ever miss it?"

Lorelei paused, wanting to give him a real answer and not just a knee-jerk response. "I love Texas. In theory. But… I don't—I've never felt like I love who I am when I'm here." She glanced up from beneath her lashes to see if he was laughing at her inane answer.

But his gaze was contemplative, as if she'd said something worth considering instead of jumbled nonsense. "You love who you are in Philadelphia?"

People didn't openly mock her there and she wasn't reminded of the parents she'd lost every time she turned a corner, so that was a start. "I excelled in college in a way I didn't going to school here. I mean, I was always good at the academic part, but I didn't quite fit in." Especially after other students went out of their way to make sure of that. "At the university, I found other people like me, people who looked up to me. In Philadelphia, I feel like someone who's got her act together, someone who's respected and is going to move up at her company."

And here, she felt like a frustrated daughter trapped in a cycle with her mother constantly disappointing each other. Although, Lorelei supposed that cycle had ended now.

She pushed her plate away. "Ever since I got here, you and other people have been telling me how special Wanda was. I don't disagree," she added quickly. "She was completely her own person, comfortable in her skin in a way I envy. She was lively and free-spirited. But being so utterly different from her…"

"Did you worry you weren't special, too?" he teased lightly.

She graced him with a half smile, appreciating his attempt to keep her from getting too maudlin. "I tried to talk to her some about how I felt, how I didn't fit in at school, how much I missed Dad. But those conversations never made me feel any closer to her. Mom lived in her own happy bubble of denial. Like the way other kids treated me was irrelevant, like Dad wasn't really gone. He just 'existed on a different plane.' I stopped coming to her because she seemed so disappointed in my outlook, my inability to be like her. In Philadelphia, I can be Lorelei without feeling like I need to apologize for it every five minutes."

Winding down, she took a deep breath. "All right. This is twice we've gone out to dinner and twice I've unloaded on you. No more, I promise." But beneath the sheepishness, she felt a glimmer of satisfaction. She'd finally managed to discuss her family, a difficult topic for her, without getting short-tempered with Sam.

"I shouldn't have been so hard on you before for not visiting her," he said. "You have to understand, from my perspective… She missed you so much. I'm not saying that to make you feel guilty," he hastily assured her. "Just so you know, however different the two of you were, she loved you. And I can actually understand staying away. My mom lives in Dallas, and there's nothing stopping me from visiting her."

"When was the last time you saw her?"

"The twins' high school graduation. She got pregnant pretty quickly after her second marriage. It was one of the reasons she gave my uncle for not rushing right back to get me. First, it was they were newlyweds and needed time to make their union a strong foundation before adding me to the mix. Then it was that she was just so overwhelmed with having two babies at once and I was better off where I was than if I were uprooted again. My half sisters seem like nice enough girls, if too superficial, but when I'm at the house… Let's just say, I know what you mean about not fitting into your own family."

She reached out and squeezed his hand. "Thank you. It's nice to think someone kind of understands, even though I wish things had been different for you."

"I don't know. Our experiences shape us," he said philosophically. "I doubt I would have been happier growing up in the country club suburb than out on the ranch with JD. And if my past had been different, I'd be different, too. I might not be the delightful person you see before you now," he deadpanned.

She guffawed at that. "Yeah, delightful is totally the first adjective that springs to mind whenever I think of you."

He raised an eyebrow. "How—" He straightened abruptly, losing his smile.

"Sam? What is it, what's wrong?"

"Nothing, really." He stifled an aggrieved groan. "It's dumb. But you know how you were saying earlier you wanted to make up for last night? Save me from that woman, and we'll be even. More than even, I'll owe you!"

Lorelei laughed, remembering how uncomfortable he'd been at the Jalapeño when she'd speculated that the waitress had a crush on him. If Sam was going to swagger around town being a sexy six-feet-plus cowboy, he had to expect a little female interest. She swiveled her head to see who had him running scared. A woman with streaked blond hair and incredibly long legs was sauntering through the crowd, a predatory expression on her striking face.

A face Lorelei suddenly recognized. "*Babs?* Oh, hell no."

"I take it you've met my stalker?"

Chapter Ten

Sam always dreaded being cornered by Barbara, partly because she was the adored younger cousin of a horse rancher who frequently gave Sam work. *And I'd miss working with those Thoroughbreds.* While Sam tried not to insult the woman outright, he brushed her off as firmly as courtesy allowed. Did she persist because she was that confident in her own charms, because she loved a challenge or because she was simply too spoiled to accept not getting something she thought she wanted?

Ironically, if Sam ever actually dated her, she'd probably dump him. Everything about the blonde screamed high-maintenance. Who spent hundreds of dollars on a pair of boots that would be ruined if you ever wore them into a barn?

Yet now, for the first time in memory, Sam felt something other than weary resignation when he spotted Barbara prowling toward him. He was curious over the sudden bright spots of color in Lorelei's cheeks. She snapped her gaze back to him and pasted a wide, patently false smile on her face.

"Stick with me, cowboy," she muttered, barely moving her lips. "I've got this covered."

He grinned. *Things just got interesting.* Lorelei once again reached for his hand, the one she'd squeezed in empathy moments ago. This time she laced her fingers through his and dropped their hands atop the bar.

"There you are, Sammy!" Barbara's voice was habitually breathless. No doubt some men found it sexy, but it always left Sam biting back the advice that if she didn't wear such tight shirts, she could probably get more oxygen. It seemed at first as if she planned to ignore Lorelei's presence entirely, but then her blue eyes narrowed on their joined hands. Barbara's smile tightened. "Aren't you going to introduce me to your friend?"

"Why, Babs!" Lorelei's voice came out far

more breathy than usual, and it was all Sam could do not to laugh at the subtle imitation. "I'm hurt you don't remember me. Lorelei Keller? We were in class together from practically kindergarten to graduation. Not that I'd expect you to remember me after so many years. High school was a lifetime ago, wasn't it?"

Barbara's nostrils flared slightly at the insinuation that they were no longer young women.

"I hear you're married now," Lorelei said brightly. "To Trace Collins, isn't it?"

"We're divorced, actually."

"After Trace, she married Vance Emmett," Sam inserted. "But they divorced, too."

"Oh." Lorelei's forehead crinkled in a sympathetic frown. "But don't you worry, sugar. Pretty gal like you is sure to find your Mr. Right! I'd love to catch up more, but Sam was just about to take me out onto the dance floor." She winked and lowered her voice to a conspiratorial woman-to-woman pitch. "And when a guy like Sam wants to hold you… well, how could I pass up that?"

Lorelei slid off her stool, her hand still clasped with his, and led him onto the floor. He immediately tugged her into his arms, loving the excuse to bring her close. Keeping one hand at her shoulder, he slid his other hand down to her waist. It took real self-discipline not to let his touch drift farther, following the tantalizing flare of her hips.

As they shuffled into a basic two-step, Sam smiled down at her, his tone full of admiration. "You are a very bad person."

"You know, I was admitting that very thing to someone this afternoon." Her brown eyes gleamed, and no matter how obviously she tried, she couldn't stifle her grin.

Sam didn't think she'd ever looked sexier as she failed to quell her unrepentant mischievousness. "Thanks for your assistance. When I asked you to save me, I didn't realize you'd throw yourself into the task with so much gusto."

There were a lot more dancers circling the wood floor than there had been when Sam and Lorelei had first arrived this evening. As they took a turn, he had to pull her tighter against him. Her chest brushed his, and he momentarily lost his rhythm in the soft press of her body. Their legs tangled, her skirt swishing against his jeans. Logically, he knew he couldn't feel it through the denim, but his skin prickled as if she'd stroked his flesh with the silky material.

"I was happy to help," Lorelei said. "Probably too happy. I didn't realize I was such a petty vindictive person. It's a little depressing, really."

"From what I know of you—and of Barbara—I'm sure she had that coming."

"Back in the day, she had a lot of not very nice things to say about me. And said equally unkind things about Wanda," she added darkly.

Well, that cinched it—Barbara's chances of winning Sam over were officially lower than the odds of a man who'd never purchased a ticket hitting the Lotto Texas jackpot. Wanda had been a nurturing soul who'd always managed to find good in people. What possible reason could someone have for running her down?

He didn't want to glance toward the bar to see if they had an audience. He'd much rather look into Lorelei's eyes. "She still there?"

Lorelei bobbed her head in the affirmative. "Glaring daggers into me over the top of her martini glass. Maybe she's changed over the years, but the Babs I remember doesn't give up easily."

"Are you saying we should try harder to dissuade her?" He steered Lorelei toward the edge of the floor, out of the path of other dancers.

"Whatever you need," Lorelei said blithely.

"I'm just here to play decoy. And, apparently, act out juvenile vengeance."

He stopped moving, steadying her when she almost stumbled. She glanced up reflexively, her brows drawing together in question. He slid the hand on her shoulder behind her neck, through the rumpled waves of her hair, and leaned down. He could actually see her pulse stutter in the hollow of her throat, hear her breathing change.

She made no move to discourage him or duck away, though. Far from it—the barely banked wickedness in her eyes blazed back to life, but there was no accompanying humor this time. Only heat.

Oh, God. Sam's about to kiss me. Shock and desire bloomed within Lorelei. And then, just like that, he *was* kissing her. Without any fumbling hesitation, his mouth had covered hers. Lorelei froze temporarily, surprised this was actually happening. It was entirely unlike her.

Was it?

She'd imagined this plenty, and now she had the opportunity to experience it first-hand. He teased his tongue over her lower lip. The sensation that quivered through her jolted her from her trance. She parted her lips, and he took the movement for the invitation it was. As their kiss deepened, Lorelei started to feel light-headed, flushed with warmth and a greedy craving for more. Sam's mouth put to shame all the wines she'd tried yesterday, intoxicating in a completely different way.

A sharp moan escaped her and she dimly registered that his palm was cupping the back of her head as if he was trying to press her closer. Which was funny, really, because she'd already voluntarily moved as close as two fully dressed people could physically be. That thought led to imagining them *not* fully dressed and sheer need stabbed through her.

Without relaxing his hold on her, Sam tilted his head back, resting his forehead on hers as they caught their breath. Lorelei was practically panting. She should probably feel embarrassed about that—they'd been making out like hormone-crazed teenagers in front of an audience! But right now the rising lust far outweighed any mortification.

Sam eyed her with a combination of awe and wariness, as if she were some dangerous temptress. "You may be bad, but you are one hell of a good kisser."

Back at you, cowboy. Her mind seemed to be in working order, but her body was still too dazed for her to form words. They just stared at each other. Lorelei didn't know how long they would have remained there, motionless, if a sudden burst of thunder hadn't made her jump. She'd completely forgotten about the storm. Which wasn't surprising, since she'd also forgotten about the roomful of people, including Barbara.

Lorelei heard herself giggle, a very unsophisticated sound.

"Please tell me you're not laughing at the way I kiss," Sam said. "The male ego is very fragile."

She rolled her eyes. "Yeah, I noticed how shy and uncertain you were. You expect me to believe women haven't already told you that you kiss like a pagan god?"

"Ah." The word was a rumble of satisfaction. "My ego thanks you. So what's funny?"

"I just don't think that when Barbara made her beeline across the bar toward you that *this* was the end result she imagined."

Sam brushed his knuckles over her cheek. "It's not exactly what I imagined, either."

Meaning that their kiss was better than what he'd envisioned, or that he never would have thought anything like this could happen between them?

"We should get off the floor," Sam said. "We're a traffic hazard."

She followed him through the crowd and back to the bar. When she attempted to settle their tab, he objected. The bartender laughingly sided with Sam. "I realize, ma'am, that in this day and age, women should be able to pay, but we're just not that enlightened here."

Maybe some feminist part of her should be annoyed, but how irritated could she be with a man who'd just kissed her senseless *and* wanted to buy her dinner? They made it to the exit without running into Barbara again, which suited Lorelei just fine. Though she'd taken an unexpectedly naughty joy in tweaking the woman earlier, right now she didn't want to be reminded that Babs had been the impetus for that soul-shaking kiss. Besides, Lorelei's brain was currently liquefied. If she got into a verbal sparring match with her former nemesis, she'd be at a loss for a single timely comeback. *High school all over again.*

Sam held open the door for her and she saw that the storm had grown worse while they'd been inside. Small hailstones littered the front walkway. The parking lot was one big mudslide.

"We could stay here," Sam mused, "but

we're under tornado watches later tonight and I'd just as soon get on the road before anyone with a few beers under their belt heads home."

"I'm game." The inn was only ten minutes away under normal conditions.

"Hang on tight," was all the warning Sam gave before swooping her up into his arms. Hurrying, he carried her through the rain toward the pickup truck.

Though Lorelei tried to maintain some discipline about diet and exercise, at five-eight she was never going to be a delicate armful. It was impossible not to be impressed with the way he cradled her. But he had to set her down to unlock the door. Holding her against the side of the truck, he let her slide down against his body. Her body tingled at the contrast between cold rain sluicing over them and the heat of him surrounding her. If they hadn't been standing in a public parking lot and lightning weren't flashing all around, she'd be tempted to brace herself against the truck and wrap her legs around his waist.

"There you go." He popped open the door. "You okay?" he asked when she didn't immediately jump in the dry shelter of the cab.

She swallowed. "Dandy." Except that she was losing her mind.

What was she doing, fantasizing about jumping a man she'd known for a week outside a bar? That scenario offered health risks, emotional risks *and* legal risks. While she wasn't one hundred percent up to date on Texas public indecency laws, she was pretty sure sex while standing in a parking lot was against code. Still, the picture of what making love to Sam might be like flashed through her mind again, and she shivered.

"You chilled?" Sam asked solicitously. "I've got the heater on, but it'll take a minute to be effective."

"Actually, I'm not as cold as you'd expect."

He half turned to her as though about to respond, but then simply shook his head and focused on peering through the windshield. There was some debris on the roads, mostly in the form of small tree branches. The silence that fell between them felt natural at first, more an attempt to concentrate on careful driving than awkwardness over his kissing her. Yet, the longer they were in the car and the more time Lorelei had to dwell on her ardent response, the more difficult it became not to say anything.

A few minutes ago, she'd been thinking about how good it would feel to have Sam inside her. And here they were on their way to a hotel where they'd be alone together all night. Did he think that when they reached the inn, they might continue where they'd left off? Mild panic fluttered in her chest. *Definitely panic.* Not *excitement, you hussy.*

She waited until he'd safely crossed a path of road covered in standing water before she broached the subject. "What I said earlier, about you kissing like a god? I meant it. That was—" Hotter than a Lone Star Fourth of July "—nice. And you know I was happy to help out with your stalker."

"But it was an isolated incident," Sam recited as if he were a student spouting memorized facts. "You're not the type of woman to be ruled by your passions, making impulsive mistakes that you'll regret when you're in a more rational mood."

"Uh, yeah." Pretty much in a nutshell. Lorelei didn't know whether to be impressed that he understood her so well or vaguely insulted. The way he described her, she sounded dull and inflexible.

"Agreed. One-time deal."

Well, that was easy. She blinked. "So you weren't planning to try and kiss me later?" At all?

He kept his eyes on the partially flooded road, but his mouth curved into a devilish grin. "Disappointed, darlin'?"

"Wh— No. I'm relieved we worked through it logically. Thank you for being so considerate of my point of view." She slumped down in her seat, proud that she and Sam, despite their brief history of hostile miscommunications, had reached such a sensible accord. Yep, she was pleased. And not at all despondent at the thought of his mouth never again taking hers.

By the time Sam pulled his truck behind the inn, the lightning had died down. But an eerie wind howled over them. Lorelei knew that tomorrow morning, the small buds that had started to blossom on flowering trees would be floating in mud puddles like soggy confetti. She just hoped the destruction would be limited to flora and fauna, not people's roofs and fences.

She and Sam filed into the kitchen and she paused at the door to the laundry room, shrugging out of the borrowed denim jacket. "I'll wash and dry this and have it back to you by tomorrow." For now, she planned to wash and dry herself. "I think I'm gonna sink into a hot bath for a little while." All of the guest rooms contained private bathrooms with shower stalls, two of which were specially equipped for handicapped visitors, but the only tub in the place was in the master suite that had been her mother's. Right now, the huge square tub sounded like heaven.

Sam nodded. "See you in the morning. And Lorelei? Thank you."

For tracking him down this afternoon to apologize? For running interference with Babs? For telling him he kissed like a god? Lorelei thought it best not to ask, since she was striving to forget just how addictive his kisses were.

She went to her room and grabbed her most comfortable nightgown, a pale yellow dress that fell to midthigh from wide shirred straps. It was her favorite because of the ultrasoft fabric, but when she'd packed it, she hadn't known she'd be sharing the inn with someone else. The sweetheart neckline and high hem were a bit more revealing than she was comfortable with Sam seeing, so she also pulled the guest robe out of the closet. She'd just finished tossing a couple of toiletry items into a duffel bag when her cell phone jangled.

"Hello?" Holding the phone between her

ear and shoulder, she gathered up her stuff and padded barefoot into the hall.

"It's Ava, dear. Please tell me you're in safe for the night and not out in this humdinger of a storm?"

Lorelei smiled into the receiver, touched by the woman's maternal concern. "Yeah, Sam and I are both—"

"And what is all this I hear about the two of you making out on the dance floor?"

The abrupt interrogation surprised Lorelei so much she nearly tripped over her own feet. "Uh…" *Word travels fast.*

She hurried down the stairs, hoping she was out of earshot of his room. It would be humiliating to get caught discussing him on the phone like some teenager dishing to a girlfriend. "He said Barbara Biggins has been stalking him, and he's had a tough time convincing her he's not interested. It was an act for her benefit." And also the most stirring kiss Lorelei had experienced in her adult life, but that wasn't relevant.

"Just an act?" There was a flat note in Ava's tone. Skepticism or disappointment?

Lorelei pushed open the door to her mother's room—she couldn't think of the suite as anything else, even after days of packing away Wanda's belongings. "He's an attractive man and a good kisser, I grant you. But it's not as if we have much in common. Including the states we live in, remember?"

"All right. Just checking. I didn't want to step on your toes when I introduce him to my niece this weekend."

Lorelei blinked. "Your niece?"

"Emily. She's a paralegal who lives in San Marcos." The city Ava mentioned was right here in the Hill Country, famed for its river and springs. "She's coming to town for the festival. Emily broke up with her fiancé last year. I didn't want to push her while she was recovering but I think she's lonely. And she's such a nice girl! You know, your mother and I always used to say Sam needed a good woman in his life."

Lorelei felt a wholly irrational twinge. Wanda had wanted to set him up with someone but had never once mentioned him to her single daughter? Of course, logically the idea of Lorelei and Sam together wouldn't have made a lick of sense, but normally that wouldn't have stopped Wanda.

In the bathroom, she found a jar of lavender-scented foaming bath salts that claimed on the label to "soothe away stress." Lorelei dumped a ton of it into the running water.

"Hello? Lorelei?"

"I'm here."

"Oh. Thought maybe the call had dropped for a second there."

She sat on the edge of the tub, sticking out her hand to check the temperature. "Ava, does Sam know you plan to shove an available woman into his path? Because he was just saying the other night that he doesn't want a relationship."

Undeterred, Ava made a dismissive *pfffft* noise. "Honey, every man says that until he meets the woman who changes his mind. He can't discount Emily if he's never even met her."

Lorelei frowned, trying to follow that reasoning.

"I am more than capable of handling Sam," Ava continued confidently. "I just wanted to make sure *you* were okay with it."

"Sure. Of course. Why wouldn't I be? Hope it all works out for those crazy kids. Look, Ava, I appreciate you checking on me, but I was just getting ready to sink into a bubble bath, so..."

"Talk to you tomorrow, then."

Lorelei set the phone on the linen shelf and undressed, wondering absently who'd tattled to Ava about the kiss. After being gone from town so long, Lorelei couldn't imagine anyone here caring what *she* did. No, she suspected Sam was the primary person of interest in any gossip that got passed along. Just because Barbara was his most aggressive admirer didn't mean dozens of other aspiring women weren't also keeping tabs on him. *Brace yourself, ladies.* They were about to have another rival for Sam's affections in kind-hearted but lonely Emily.

She clipped her hair up into a haphazard knot. Tendrils of steam beckoned from the bubble-filled tub and Lorelei sank into the water with a contented sigh. Her body had been thrumming with electric tension ever since Sam put his arms around her on the dance floor. Now, her muscles finally started to loosen. She closed her eyes, only to have them pop open again when she heard a sound at the door.

"Hello?" She cocked her head and realized that the noise was scratching. A paw batted from beneath the door, insistently demanding entrance. Lorelei recalled her mom saying that when she brushed her teeth in the mornings and evenings, Oberon liked to follow her into the bathroom and sit on the vanity, mewing conversationally as if he were telling her about his plans or recapping his day.

Should've closed the outer door. Though she'd locked the bathroom door, she'd been preoccupied by her conversation with Ava and hadn't closed the door between the bedroom and the rest of the house.

"Sorry, Obie," she muttered. "I bathe alone."

The scratching became more frantic, and she flicked a handful of water at floor level, hoping that if his paw got wet, he'd retreat. Instead, as if she'd declared war, he retaliated with a shrill battle cry that made the hairs on the back of her neck rise. Lorelei found herself wondering if Lonely Emily might like a cat for company.

"Go away," she insisted.

She wanted to believe she could simply ignore him, but Oberon did not accept defeat. Any minute now, he'd launch into a peace-shattering caterwaul. Not willing to cede her serenity to a freaking feline, she stood. She grabbed her towel off the brass hook and wrapped it around her. She planned to boot his fuzzy butt from the room and shut the master suite door. Let him yowl out in the hallway—she'd turn on some music before resuming her bath.

When she opened the bathroom door, Oberon took off like a shot. But she didn't doubt he'd try to return. Time to shut the door and flip on the radio. Lorelei had only taken two more steps toward the door when the entire inn was plunged into blackness. There was also a jolting silence as appliances and ceiling fans stopped functioning. She stood still, waiting for her eyes to adjust before she tried to find a candle or matches. Blundering around in the darkness could lead to her stubbing a toe on a piece of furniture or tripping over the cat.

But before she'd had a chance to reorient herself, a beam of light flashed down the hall and Sam rounded the corner, stopping short at the sight of her in a towel. She blinked against the brightness.

His voice was hoarse. "Power..." He coughed into his fist, tried again. "The power went out."

"I noticed." She shifted her weight, careful not to drop the towel, hyperaware of the suds dripping along her collarbone and the fact that her topknot was flopping limply to the side of her head.

Sam took a step closer, flipping the flashlight away so it wasn't shining directly at her. "Here. You might need this."

"Thanks." Tightening her grip on the towel with one hand, she reached out the other one, grateful but perplexed. "How'd you get here so fast with a light?" It was as if he'd just been hanging out in the hallway, waiting for them to lose electricity.

"I was on the way already and grabbed the emergency flashlight out of the outlet where it was charging. I thought I heard you shriek. I was afraid you might have hurt yourself or seen a critter." He gestured to the towel she wore. "I would've knocked before I came in."

The image that sprang to Lorelei's mind was in direct contrast to his words. She could too easily picture herself reclining in the bubbly water when suddenly the door opened…

She swallowed. "You came to save me from a potential critter? I live alone in Philly," she reminded him, unused to anyone riding to her rescue. "I've had to deal with critters on my own."

"Yeah." His lips twitched. "But everything's bigger in Texas."

Unbidden, her gaze slid down his body. When she caught herself, she yanked her eyes back up, hoping it was too dark for him to have noticed. But he was staring so intently she doubted she could hide anything from him. He reached out a hand as if in slow motion and brushed away a line of frothy soap that had been winding toward the towel and the crevice between her breasts. Lorelei's breath caught. Why hadn't she tried harder to talk Ava out of any misbegotten matchmaking attempts? *Maybe I should warn him. As his friend.*

But she couldn't quite dredge up the nerve to discuss Sam's love life while she stood there wearing no clothes. "That noise you heard wasn't me. Oberon was throwing a tantrum because he was locked out. He wanted to keep me company while I was in the tub."

Sam smirked. "Then he—"

Click, whir. Light poured through the room. Lorelei gasped, her towel slipping a couple of centimeters before she caught the top of it. Sam's expression was so deliciously predatory that she was torn between fleeing and letting the towel hit the hardwood.

Backing away, she stammered, "I—I should finish rinsing off now."

He nodded. "Maybe I'll go take a shower, too." As he turned the corner, she heard him mumble, "A very cold one."

Chapter Eleven

The kickoff day for the festival, Saturday, also happened to be St. Patrick's Day. Irish or not, luck was definitely with the town. The day dawned clear and bright, all of the week's previous storms having rolled through. The sky was a brilliant blue and although the early morning hours were cool enough to warrant a sweater, temperatures were forecast to reach the high seventies by noon. After spending much of Friday indoors with bankers and real estate agents, Lorelei looked forward to being outside today.

Tess Fitzpatrick, who had generously come over last night to help fill giveaway bags with calming incense and potpourri, promised to stop by the booth during downtimes when she wasn't organizing pint-size dancers for their next show. From her spot on the spacious public lawn, Lorelei watched dancers from the high school stretch and a group of musicians set up their instruments and sheet music. Lorelei was situated between a trio of women selling handmade jewelry and a middle-aged couple who were unpacking boxes of jars. Closer inspection revealed the jars were full of marinade, including one made with red wine from a local vineyard and another that was intriguingly labeled "madman moonshine marinade."

Lorelei knew her version of the Haunted Hill Country booth wasn't quite what her mother would have done, yet she felt Wanda would approve. To honor her mother's lifelong faith in pig figures as lucky talismans, Ava and Lorelei had found a novelty tablecloth—probably meant for BBQ events—that was covered in smiling pigs. Lorelei had also put together a scrapbook celebrating the inn and surrounded it with pamphlets on some of the area's other B and Bs, spotlighting those her mom had liked the best. And Lorelei had printed and folded the brochures saved on her mom's PC that offered advice on dealing with Hill Country spirits.

Included were a reminder never to slam doors (lest you injure a ghost crossing the threshold and antagonize it into haunting you); the reassurance that most ghosts are benign but should you run across one you'd like to shake, try imitating a rooster's crow (the specter may fade away if it believes dawn is breaking); and the advice to turn your pockets inside out whenever passing a graveyard (to keep the spirits from sneaking into your pockets and hitching a ride).

At festivals past, Wanda had playfully attempted "readings," either through cards or tea leaves. Lorelei refused to go that far to entertain booth visitors, but she had purchased a large bag of fortune cookies at a party supply store in a neighboring county. She'd filled a green plastic bowl with the cookies and set it among the goodie bags.

She'd just finished reassuring a little girl in a flashing shamrock necklace that the cookies were free when she looked up and saw a familiar bearded face. Dwayne, the would-be ghost hunter, angled two fingers at her in wry salute. Today, sitting out in the cheery sunshine at a display table that reminded her how enthusiastic Wanda had been about the supernatural, Lorelei wished she'd handled Dwayne and his friend with more benevolence.

"Hi," she called.

His auburn brows rose but after a moment, he ambled toward her. "Hello. Mind if I take one of these pamphlets?" He gestured to her stack of Hill Country spirits brochures.

"Please do." She handed him two, including one for his friend. "I don't want to have to take all these back with me at the end of the day. Is your buddy here, too?" she asked, scanning the crowd.

"Jerry." Dwayne nodded. "He's over by the water wheel, interviewing a man who's lived here all his life. Man claims that his twin brother died in 2002 but always visits on their birthday."

Lorelei thought she kept her expression neutral, but Dwayne cocked his head, studying her as if he'd seen a flash of something.

"You really hate this paranormal stuff, huh?"

She leaned back in her folding chair. "*Hate* is a strong word."

"But accurate?" he persisted.

"My mom was really into it. I guess I just..."

He held up his hands. "Say no more. Both of my parents are into surgery. Performing it, not getting it done. They wanted me to go to medical school. Not my thing, though."

She tried to picture him in a white coat and consulting a patient file but failed spectacularly. "Well, even though ghosts aren't my thing—largely because I think it's all bunk—I didn't mean to go ballistic on you guys the other day."

He grinned at her. "Right before we left, you *did* look like you were going to shoot lasers out of your eyes. Kinda terrifying. It was our bad, though. I was all hyped up on energy drinks and should have been more compassionate. Forgive me?"

"If you'll forgive my wigging out."

"Done." He winked. "Besides, me and Jerry like scary entities."

That made her chuckle and she was still smiling when Sam approached her table. His green button-down shirt made his eyes sparkle like emeralds beneath the brim of his cowboy hat.

"You look like you're enjoying yourself," he said. "Didn't I just see that guy we ran off from the inn the other day?"

"Dwayne. He stopped by to grab some pamphlets and tell me I was scary."

"He's got that right," Sam drawled.

"Hey!" She reached out to swat him on the arm, and he grabbed her hand.

"You're supposed to be wearing green today," he said, his voice stern with mock-reprimand.

She tried not to be distracted by his continuing to hold her hand. "This is green." *Ish.* She'd paired a lace-trimmed sweater with a short black skirt.

"No, it's one of those weird not-quite-blue colors only women know the names of. Turquoise or something."

Teal. When she'd packed a suitcase for Texas, she'd been in shock over her mother's death. The last thing she'd considered was the upcoming St. Patrick's Day and whether she'd be in town that long.

"Tradition says you could get pinched," he continued.

She arched an eyebrow. "Try it and die, cowboy."

His only response was a wolfish smile.

She snatched her hand back. "Aren't you supposed to be busy roping dogies?" As in, *get along little?* He was working over at the fairgrounds today, participating in interactive demonstrations of roping and saddling.

"Headed that way now," he said. "Just thought I'd say hi first." He turned to blend into the crowd but only got a few vendors away before he stopped, exchanged greetings with an elderly woman and leaned down to pick up something off the table. Then he pivoted and retraced his steps to Lorelei.

He crooked his finger at her with a grin. “C’mere.” He leaned across the table, and she met him halfway. He dropped two strands of bright green shamrock-bead necklaces over her head, letting his hands slide down over her. His breath was warm against her ear as he murmured, “There. Now you’re safe.”

Interesting word choice. Lorelei had always associated “safe” with security and seat belts and comfy socks— not a spike of adrenaline at the feeling of a man’s touch and the giddy uncertainty of whether he might kiss her again.

As he walked away, she tried not to appear overtly fascinated with his jeans. But her admiration was echoed in a hearty sigh behind her.

“*Mmm,* that man. You are a lucky lady,” Tess said.

Lorelei turned to smile at the redhead. “Hey, Tess.”

The woman shrugged a large macramé purse off her shoulder and set it under the table. She was wearing a white tennis skirt with a dark green polo and had accessorized the outfit with green polka-dotted suspenders and lime-colored canvas shoes. She looked like the peppy head cheerleader for Leprechaun U.

"Very cute," Lorelei said.

"Thanks. I had considered just wearing a green leotard and tights under a sandwich board that said, 'Kiss Me, I'm Irish,' but thought that might be a touch desperate." She plopped into the other folding chair. "If I weren't so eternally grateful to you for helping me understand geometry proofs, I might have to hate you. I've been depressingly single for the past six months and, in a single week back, you snagged the interest of Sam Travis." She grabbed one of the B-and-B brochures off the table and fanned herself dramatically.

Lorelei looked away, nibbling on her bottom lip. It was one thing to act as Sam's human shield where Barbara was concerned, but Lorelei was usually honest to a fault. Painfully blunt, she'd been called. Letting Tess, who'd been so genuinely kind to her, believe something untrue discomfited her.

"There's not anything between me and Sam, not really. It's just a matter of close quarters while we're both staying at the inn."

"Y'all may not be picking out china patterns, but he was interested enough to kiss you in front of everyone over at the Star the other night. That's further than most women around here have gotten with him." Tess's brown eyes twinkled. "And trust me, plenty have tried."

Lorelei laughed. "That I can believe. So he really hasn't dated much?"

"A woman here or there about a year ago, but nothing that ever lasted past a few dates, far as I know. Since he doesn't live here full-time, I can't say he doesn't have a steady girl *somewhere,* but if that were the case, he would have said so. He's turned Barbara Biggins away more than once. Hell, if I were him, I might have lied about having a girlfriend in parts unknown just to throw Barbara off the scent."

Lorelei sat forward, elbows on her knees, and lowered her voice to a confidential whisper. "That's why he kissed me—to con Barbara into thinking we were together."

"Really? Outstanding." Tess rubbed her hands together. "Wish I could have seen her face. She was the quintessential mean girl back in school and has not improved with age. Still, I'm kind of bummed about you and Sam. Rather, the fact that there is no you and Sam."

"Bummed? Two minutes ago you were acting jealous and implied my being with him was reason enough to hate me."

"True. But the two of you would make a very cute couple."

"We'd make a very *temporary* couple," Lorelei corrected. "As you said, Sam doesn't make his home here. Neither do I. He's a good-looking guy—"

"And a good kisser?" Tess prompted. "Tell me he's as good as he seems like he'd be."

Better. "People don't have relationships based on that." Not successful ones, anyway.

"Maybe not relationships. But people have had flings based on less," Tess said matter-of-factly.

Lorelei choked back a laugh. "I'm not the flinging type."

No, she was apparently the solitary type. This friendly bantering with Tess heightened her awareness of how few people she'd spoken to from Philadelphia in the past few days. The office receptionist had emailed condolences, on behalf of the entire staff, and Lorelei had talked to Celia a number of times—until the woman had started dodging Lorelei's micromanaging phone calls.

She'd been here over a week. Weren't there

people who were worried about her, people she should be missing more? Lorelei sometimes went jogging with one of her neighbors, and the woman had texted her that morning to say she'd just achieved her personal best for a 5K. When they did their cool-down laps, they had no trouble making small talk, but it wasn't as if Lorelei had thought of calling the woman when she was upset over picking up Wanda's ashes. Rick left a voice mail that he'd been given tickets to a sold-out show and to let him know ASAP whether she'd be home by the date of the performance—otherwise, he'd find someone else to take.

The closest thing she had to a romantic relationship boiled down to first right of refusal of theater tickets? She couldn't work up any rancor over it, though. It wasn't as if she'd been pining for Rick. With an inward sigh, she realized that when she got back to Philly, she should break the habit of doing things with him. Their convenient friendship was never going to develop into anything deeper. What if their constant partnering at events prevented them from meeting potential lovers?

Before now, Lorelei hadn't been seeking more intimacy in her life. Yet a burgeoning sense of longing was beginning to take shape.

As devoted as she was to her job, work wasn't everything. It might be nice to have a man in her life who listened to her talk about her day, who made her laugh, who had broad shoulders she could lean on, were she ever so inclined. *A man whose kisses make me dizzy.*

She was grateful for the distraction when several tourists came by the table, expressing their regret that they'd never been able to stay at the B and B, which they thought had a "cool theme." They asked her about some of the superstitions in the pamphlet and Tess joined in with some of the folklore tidbits she'd heard growing up. The women from the jewelry table came over to snag a couple of the miniature bags of potpourri, followed by a man who introduced himself as an official photographer for the event and asked Lorelei to smile for the camera. As Tess excused herself to organize a line of preschool-age tap dancers, a proprietor from one of the inns across town came over to say how glad she was Lorelei had decided to include the Haunted Hill Country booth one last time.

"It's like Wanda is here with us, saying goodbye," the woman said affectionately.

Lorelei had spent what felt like a solid two hours talking to people. It wasn't until she hit a lull and had a moment to herself that the surrounding scents really penetrated her conscious mind. Lunchtime was approaching, and the food vendors were doing a brisk business. She breathed in the buttery ears of corn, the smoky fragrance of giant roasted turkey legs, the nearly eye-watering sharpness of hot peppers and the nutty malt aroma of beer being poured into souvenir steins. Her stomach gurgled.

That's it. The booth is officially closed for lunch. She made sure the stacks of paper were weighted down with some of Wanda's topaz crystals and small chakra stones and left the fortune cookies and incense out where people could help themselves. Then she hoisted her purse and texted Tess to see if the woman wanted to meet up in one of the food pavilions.

Now that she'd realized how hungry she was, Lorelei didn't know where to start. Booths stretched across the entire length of Main Street. She grinned, suddenly very grateful that the festival spanned a week. As much as she looked forward to tomorrow's chili cook-off, for now, she decided she was in the mood for German cuisine. After piling a plate with brats, potato salad and dilled cu-

cumbers, she got a message from Tess saying We have a table, saved you a seat.

Sure enough, as soon as Lorelei entered the designated pavilion, she saw Ava standing and waving. Also present were Ava's husband, Clinton, a young woman with hair so pale it was almost white, Tess, Sam and another man in a cowboy hat. Once she was closer, she took in details of the other man's outfit, from the feathers in the band of his hat to the longhorn skull pattern on his colorful shirt to his bolo tie and a gold belt buckle that probably weighed more than Oberon. *He shouldn't sit next to Sam,* she thought almost pityingly. The man looked like some demented cliché of a "Texas cowboy" while Sam was emphatically, quietly, the real thing.

Sam stood and pulled out the chair between him and Tess.

"Thank you." It occurred to Lorelei that she was going to get spoiled here and would need to remember how to open her own doors and scoot back her own chairs when she left.

"Lorelei, this is my niece, Emily Hirsch," Ava said, introducing a pretty woman with a too-solemn expression. Her stick-straight platinum hair was held off her face by a wide red band, and her high cheekbones were better defined than words in a dictionary.

"Nice to meet you," Lorelei said, her imagination preoccupied with the idea of this woman and Sam. Did Emily seem perhaps a bit too frail and ethereal for him, a man who worked with his hands and tromped through mud and rain with no umbrella?

"We've been meaning to come by your booth all morning," Ava said apologetically. "We just haven't made it that far yet."

"Aunt Ava must know everyone in town," Emily said, sounding awed. "She can't go three feet without someone stopping us to hug her or ask her opinion on something."

"If you two get a chance, stop by after lunch," Lorelei invited them. "You can tell me any ghost anecdotes you know. I'm tired of repeating the same three over and over."

Ava shook her head. "Have you asked Sam for help? He's the tour guide for the 'haunted' trail ride, for pete's sake. You should see him spellbind the tourists with stories."

Lorelei shot him a sidelong glance. When he was in one of his reticent moods, it was impossible to picture him as an engaging storyteller. But this morning, when he'd teased her about wearing the wrong color, his face had been so expressive, a pure joy to watch. And when he'd brought her that flashlight during the inn's power outage, his voice had been husky enough to make her shiver. There would be worse ways to spend an evening than sidled up to a campfire listening to that voice.

Ava had turned to Sam, her cheerful tone bordering on manic energy. "Emily here is a storyteller, too! She volunteers twice a month at a library, working with kids. I just know you'll make a great mother someday," Ava told her niece warmly.

Lorelei almost winced at the uncomfortable expression on Emily's face. The paralegal was squirming in her chair, obviously wishing her aunt would stop her matchmaking attempts—or at least be more subtle about them. For his part, Sam had hunkered down over his plate, attacking his food with a single-minded ruthlessness, as if eating would give him a socially acceptable excuse for ignoring conversation altogether.

In an attempt to dispel the awkwardness, Lorelei interrupted Ava's rhapsodies by turning to the man with the belt buckle. "I'm sorry, but I don't think we've met."

"Dickie Gebhart at your service, ma'am. I manage one of the clothing stores here in town."

"One of the Western wear emporiums?" she asked.

His smile flashed white beneath his dark mustache. "What gave it away?"

"Speaking of clothes—" Ava turned to her niece "—you have to go shopping with me while you're in town. Emily has such an eye for color and detail. Why, when Clinton and I decided a couple of years ago to redecorate, Emily practically designed the new living room for us. Didn't she, Clinton?"

"Uh-huh." Clinton dutifully nodded his gray head without ever looking up from his spaetzle.

Lorelei resisted the urge to smack her forehead with her palm. Ava was a very dear woman—looking back, Lorelei wasn't sure how she would have survived this week without her—but as a Cupid, she lacked finesse. After Tess gave an humorous recap of one of the morning's dances, Ava launched into a memory of one of Emily's recitals, her proud tone suggesting that Emily could have been a prima ballerina if she hadn't chosen to be a paralegal instead. Ava didn't seem to notice that her niece was looking at her as if she were off her meds.

"Aunt Ava, I only took dance for six months.

Because Mom made me. I was *horrible* at it, hated every minute. Two left feet," the woman confided across the table to Tess.

This news inordinately cheered Lorelei. Sam was an excellent dancer. It seemed that Ava might be grasping at straws in thinking Emily and Sam were compatible.

While they were clearing the table at the end of the meal, Sam remarked on Lorelei's mood. "What's got you so happy?" he asked as they carried their trays to a nearby trash bin. "You're whistling."

"Was I? Guess I've just had a lot of fun today." That was true. She'd enjoyed it more than she could have predicted. Even Ava being a little bit kooky had a certain rightness to it, reminding Lorelei of her eccentric mother. "I miss Mom."

Sam stared at her, uncomprehending. "Okay. See, that sounds like a sad statement. Missing her put you in a good mood?"

"No. I just… I feel close to her here. I'm really grateful you convinced me to do this."

"Grateful enough to help me fake my own death and get into some kind of witness protection program? Ava has lost her ever lovin' mind."

Lorelei smothered a laugh. "Don't worry.

I'll protect you from the oh-so-scary retired lady and her pretty niece."

Instead of acting offended by her mild ridicule, Sam surprised her by dropping a kiss on top of her head. "Thanks, darlin'. I knew I could count on you."

After accepting a ride from Tess, Lorelei arrived at the inn shortly after sundown. Oberon met her at the door with his best woe-is-the-neglected-cat impression. She'd sorted through the mail and was filling a glass of ice water when Sam came through the back door.

He hefted a brown paper sack. "I hit a few stalls on the way to my truck—figured both of us would be too tired to cook tonight."

Lorelei groaned. "No more food. Ever." But a moment later, she heard herself ask, "Just out of curiosity, though, what did you bring?"

Laughing, he carried his bounty over to the table and began pulling out various cartons. Lorelei took a seat to better inspect the offerings, but she doubted she could eat anytime soon. This afternoon, Ava had worked a couple of hours at Wanda's table so that Emily could "hang around someone her own age," leaving Lorelei and the quiet blonde free to sample lots of festival snacks. After a few stymied attempts at conversation that went nowhere, they seemed to have reached a mutual unspoken agreement that as long as they were eating, they weren't required to speak.

Lorelei grinned at a sudden memory, thinking there was one person out there tonight who should feel even more stuffed than she was. "I kept spotting this same family throughout the day," she told Sam. "They had the cutest little boy, probably around three years or four years old, and you wouldn't believe this kid's appetite! I swear every time I saw him, he was devouring something almost as big as he was—an entire sausage on a stick, a ginormous ice cream cone. Tess and I passed them on our way out. The kid had a pear in one hand and a bag of gourmet nuts in the other. God help those parents and their grocery bill when he hits his teen years!"

Rampant appetite and ice cream smears around his mouth aside, he really had been an adorable little boy. Lorelei didn't normally think of herself as a "kid person," but she'd found herself smiling at quite a few in the crowd.

"I might want to have a baby," she said, testing out how the words sounded and felt—

more an exploratory statement than a declaration.

Sam shot back in his seat so hard the chair skidded on the tile. "Uh…"

She rolled her eyes. He acted as if she'd just suggested getting pregnant tonight. "Get a grip. That wasn't my bizarre attempt at a come on. I was just realizing for the first time I might actually want kids someday in the far flung future. Unclench." Did he have any idea how panicked his expression was?

"Right. I knew that. Congratulations. In advance," he said weakly.

"You know, up until now, I've thought it was kind of funny how you avoid women and, by extension, commitment, but this is starting to seem a little pathological. Does the thought of having a family really rattle you that much?"

Instead of shrugging off her question with a macho denial that he could be scared, he shrugged. "There was a small barn at the edge of property where JD and I worked, more like a shed, really, and we cornered the occasional copperhead inside. Whenever I had to go in there for some reason, I'd get this nauseous kind of dread. I got nothing against the institution of marriage in the abstract but pondering myself with an actual wife and kids? Well. I have a venom extractor in the first-aid kit in the truck, should I ever need it, but family's a permanent condition."

She crossed her arms over her chest. "I don't buy it, the whole desperado loner vibe. You had a soft spot for Mom and you were annoyed I didn't visit her more. You do have a sense of family obligation."

"Wanda was a good woman, good to me, and I liked her. But I saw how much she missed you, how wounded she was that you weren't closer. And now that I've gotten to know you better, I see that you've got wounds of your own. Family does that. Why create more obligation for yourself and the potential for hurting one another?"

"I know your parents disappointed you," she said, softening her tone when she imagined the one-two punch of losing a father only to be abandoned by his mom. "But you got along with your uncle, right?"

"Sure. JD did his best by me. He's dead now." Sam said it simply, without a trace of self-pity, but his point was made. JD was just one more loss he'd suffered. The actuary in her completely identified with Sam's position; deeper entanglements equaled more risk. Wasn't she a believer in safeguarding oneself however possible?

Lorelei felt guilty for even pursuing the argument. What business was it of hers if Sam preferred to stay a bachelor? Yet once again, she thought of that laughing, pink-cheeked preschooler she'd seen today who'd looked so much like his own adoring father. It took shockingly little imagination for her to imagine an equally cute boy riding *Sam's* tall shoulders, mischievous eyes shining the way Sam's had this morning when he'd razzed her about not wearing the right shade of green.

She shook herself out of her reverie. Maybe this was just her heretofore unknown biological clock buzzing at her—next time she'd smack the snooze button and ignore the damn thing. "So I'm out of fortune cookies," she said, clumsily changing the subject. "I was surprised by how many people asked me about fortune-telling or reading their auras or whatever. One woman came by the table to specifically invite me to her house for a Ouija board attempt at getting in touch with Mom. I'm going to have to come up with something for tomorrow."

"What, you mean like taking a crystal ball to the booth with you?" he asked, an unmaterialized grin flirting around the corners of his mouth.

"I was thinking more along the lines of printing out tomorrow's horoscopes and reading the pertinent signs to anyone interested."

"Guess that's technically more interactive than the fortune cookies," he said dubiously. "But it lacks showmanship."

"Sorry. We weren't all born with your inherent skill for hamming it up in front of crowds, Mr. In-The-Center-Ring." Despite her teasing tone, she'd been impressed when she and Emily had caught one of Sam's lasso demonstrations this afternoon.

His talent and focus were…sexy, she admitted to herself. He'd shown intense concentration on what he was doing but at the same time a total awareness of the crowd, playing to them with his smiles and his tricks. After that display and Ava's earlier remarks about him telling stories around a campfire, Lorelei was starting to look forward to their trail ride. She and Sam spent so much time alone together, it was a revelation of sorts to watch him relate to an audience. Then again, was it really a surprise that Monosyllable Man could charm folks when he wanted? After all, it wasn't the general population that spooked him, it was one-on-one connections.

"I could give you tips," he offered in a lazy drawl.

"Thanks, but no matter how good you are, I don't think you can teach me roping by tomorrow."

"Not what I had in mind. You should try your *hand* at palm reading." He emphasized his pun by waggling his fingers at her.

"Ugh," she complained. "That was beneath you."

"You didn't like the joke?"

"It's only a 'joke' if it's funny, Travis."

In response, she got the full-on grin this time instead of just the hint of one. Her toes curled inside her black ankle boots.

"For palm reading," he told her, "you don't need any of the props. Wanda had fun with her mystical cards and stuff, but you'd just be uncomfortable."

"I'll be uncomfortable anyway," she groused. "I am not holding hands with strangers all day and pretending to see the future in the wrinkles of their skin."

"It's not that bad." He held out his hand. "Here."

"You want me to pretend to read your palm?"

"Other way around. I was going to demonstrate."

She extended her arm, feeling dumb but playing along. The sights and sounds of the festival had invigorated her; the idea of retreating alone to her room wasn't nearly as enticing as sharing this lighthearted moment with Sam.

He traced light circles over her wrist with his thumb, and pleasure rippled through her. *What is wrong with you?* Hands were not erogenous zones. Or maybe they were—it had been so long since she'd had sex, she probably wouldn't remember. Then he smoothed his thumb over her palm, peering at her with mock intensity. A lock of hair fell across his face, making him boyishly enticing. For a second, she could forget that he was a jaded man who seemed to think poisonous snake bites were preferable to letting someone get close to him.

His touch feather-light, he followed a line on her palm. Her eyes closed involuntarily.

"This is your wealth line," he told her quietly.

She played along. "And do you see lots of money in my future?"

"Is money the kind of wealth that's important to you? I see you rich in other areas—rich in intelligence, the respect of your peers, the affection of your friends. And the total devotion of your husband."

Her eyes popped open. "There's a husband?"

"Definitely. Your wealth line intersects with your love line. You'll meet him soon after your return to Philadelphia. At a coffee shop. He'll bump into you and spill hot espresso down your skirt—"

"Be still my beating heart," she said drily.

"—and you, of course, will rip his head off for not watching where he was going. Luckily, he has a thing for passionate brunettes and he buys you dinner to make up for his clumsiness. A great new Italian place, where he tells you that he works for the IRS, which intimidates most women but not you. You're married within a year and have three brown-eyed children who are all able to ace the math portion of the SAT by the time they're twelve."

She drew her hand back. "Very informative. Thank you." Aside from the three kids—she was just starting to adjust to the idea of one or two—the fantasy would have sounded pretty good a week ago.

She found herself unenthusiastic about the

Italian restaurant. Because she was so full, or because she suddenly had a newfound appreciation for hole-in-the-wall Mexican fusion restaurants? And the IRS agent didn't sound as appealing as he once would have, either. In fact, Sam's entire silly prediction left her feeling a bit depressed.

Or maybe that was just the hormonal letdown after being inexplicably aroused while he was touching her hands.

"Now you have to do me." He flopped his hand down on the table. "What do you see?"

A man who had a lot to offer but who wasn't going to let himself believe that.

She slid her fingers around his and stared down, then rubbed her temple with her free hand as if she were receiving a psychic message. "Oh! Well…this is a surprise. To the shock of pretty much everyone, Barbara Biggins wears you down. You fall madly in love and have eight children. You meant to stop with five, but then came the triplets," she said sweetly.

He snatched his hand away, recoiling in horror. "Throw some salt over your shoulder or something, woman!"

"I didn't want it to sound too on-the-nose,"

she said, defending herself. "I thought I'd go for the unexpected."

"Sheesh." His green eyes were reproving. "If you don't want to marry the IRS guy, just say no when he proposes. Don't shoot the messenger."

She gave a hollow laugh as she stood. "You are a nut. And I…think I'm going to turn in early. Good night, Sam."

"Sweet dreams," he called after her.

His words bothered her because, with her skin still tingling from his simple caresses, she feared her dreams would be very enjoyable, indeed. And Lorelei eschewed dreams in favor of reality. She always felt better after taking stock of the situation and assessing the bare facts.

So, reality check. You will be gone within a week and even if you were staying, Sam wouldn't want you.

Oh, yeah. Now she felt *much* better.

Although Frederick-Fest ran all week—and tourists kept coming each day—the hours for general booths weren't as long once the weekend was over. And after all, it wasn't as if Lorelei was trying to drum up business for the inn. So by midweek, she'd pretty much packed up shop and was using her time to either make plans with her newly hired real estate agent or enjoy the festival.

On Wednesday, there was a public cooking demonstration featuring the four finalists in the televised chef competition. Lorelei spent a few minutes beforehand chatting with Grace Torres, but could tell the chef was frazzled by the pressures of trying to win this contest. As Lorelei watched from the crowd of onlookers, someone lightly grasped her elbow.

"Got a minute?" Ava whispered.

Not wanting to distract the chefs, Lorelei ambled off to the side, motioning for Ava to follow.

"What can I do for you?" Lorelei asked.

The older woman fiddled with her glasses, looking sheepish. "It's not for me, it's for Em."

Lorelei heaved a sigh at the mention of Ava's niece. "Oh, honestly. You're not still trying—"

"No! Definitely not. Sam's been avoiding me for days, and Emily gave me quite an earful Sunday night. I suppose I shouldn't have meddled. It was a long shot that they'd take to each other. It's just difficult, to love someone and see them squander their potential for happiness. It's like, ever since she ended things with that pig of an ex-fiancé, she's afraid to even try."

Despite herself, Lorelei sympathized. She recalled the look on Sam's face when he'd maintained he was better off alone. Didn't he have any idea how happy he could make the right woman—how happy said woman might make *him?*

"It's okay, Ava. I understand why you were behaving like a lunatic."

Grinning, the woman thumped Lorelei on the shoulder. "Smart aleck."

"So if you're not trying to foist Emily on Sam and vice versa, what is it that you need?"

"Today's her last day of vacation. She's going back to San Marcos after lunch tomorrow. And I'm not sure she's had a very good time, which is partly my fault. I thought maybe people closer to her age could take her out, show her some of the nightlife."

Recalling the blonde's expression when she mentioned her two left feet, Lorelei decided dancing was out of the question.

"Did you already have plans tonight?" Ava asked. "I know you and Sam have been getting ready for that camping trip." She'd agreed to come by and take care of the cat for the two days they'd be gone.

"I'm free tonight. But are you sure Emily will want to do something with me?" Lorelei didn't want to mention how awkward the girl had been while they toured the festival Saturday and again during the chili tastings on Sunday. But surely Ava must know how painfully shy her niece was? Frankly, Lorelei was a bit surprised Emily had managed to get engaged to someone in the first place.

"If you extend the invitation, I think she'll accept." Ava's cheeks reddened. "I don't want her to feel like I put you up to this."

"Got it."

In the past two weeks, Ava had been there for Lorelei in countless little ways, and Lorelei was actually glad to have an opportunity to return the kindness. It occurred to her that, assuming all went smoothly with the sale of the inn, Lorelei might not see her mother's friend after this week. Oh, they'd exchange Christmas cards and maybe the occasional email. But Lorelei's entire goal had been to put her past in Fredericksburg *behind* her. She had no plans to visit. And as far as she knew, Ava hadn't set foot in Philadelphia a single time since the fall Lorelei had gone away to college.

A knot of emotion rose in Lorelei's throat.

Acting on impulse, she threw her arms around Ava and hugged her tight.

"Uh… Lorelei?" A second passed, then Ava returned the hug, patting her lightly on the back.

"I'll miss you when I leave," Lorelei mumbled. "I hope Emily visits you a lot. Someone needs to check on you and keep you out of trouble."

Ava laughed. "That might be a bigger job than one person can handle, dear."

Releasing her hold on the other woman, Lorelei promised, "I'll come up with something for tonight and give Emily a call." Ava had passed along her niece's cell phone number a couple of days ago.

Lorelei decided that Tess would be a valuable resource to consult. After all, Tess knew a lot more about the local "nightlife" than Lorelei did. Hopefully the cheerful redhead could come with them. There wasn't a single intimidating thing about Tess; maybe she could help coax Emily from her paralyzing shyness.

Today, Tess was working in a face-painting booth where children could have their face whimsically decorated for free. "We can't charge them, or we'd end up having to refund everyone," Tess had joked last night. "Every animal I draw somehow ends up with a grotesquely long neck. Even my ladybugs look like giraffes! And don't even ask me what my attempt at the state of Texas resembled."

As Lorelei stood behind a group of children and watched her friend apply a misshapen pink blob on a little girl's cheek, she had to concede Tess's point. It was a good thing the woman made her career in the performing arts, because she seemed to have no aptitude whatsoever in the field of visual arts. Still, Lorelei wanted to be encouraging.

The pig-tailed girl admired herself in a hand mirror, then slid off her stool to rejoin her waiting parents. None of the other kids rushed to vacate the empty seat.

Lorelei stepped forward, telling Tess in a stage whisper, "I particularly liked the glittery sparkles you added to her…unicorn?"

"Close. Butterfly."

Huh. "Maybe you ought to stick to simple shapes like smiley faces and the Lone Star flag," Lorelei suggested.

A woman who was cleaning off brushes and small sponges at the other end of the long table said, "Whoever you are, tell me you came to help!"

"Not exactly." Lorelei doubted she'd be much better at this than her friend. "I actually just wanted to talk to Tess for a minute, but I can wait if you guys are too busy."

The woman sighed. "Take her. Petey Kendall is next and I can tell you from experience he's gonna want a T-Rex."

A boy standing nearby tried unsuccessfully to blow a bubble with his purple gum. "A T-Rex for the right cheek and a stegosaurus on the left!" His Witte Museum T-shirt also featured dinosaurs.

Tess tossed her arms up in defeat. "We're officially outside my skill set, so—"

"*What* skill set?" the other woman demanded.

"—I think it's time for my break. Wanna get some food?"

Lorelei laughed. "All we've done for days on end is get food!"

"That's not true." Tess sniffed. "At the vintner lecture on Monday, I also got libations."

The two of them took a lazy stroll around the playground, smiling at children's antics as they passed.

"So what did you need to talk about?" Tess asked. "And please let it be that you came to ask for my expertise in the art of seduction."

Lorelei snorted. "You consider yourself an expert?"

"Not the point. Do you realize you're leaving after this weekend and that you've yet to make a move on Sam?"

"That's because I have no intentions of making a move."

"But your chances of a mind-blowing vacation fling are dwindling! Staying under the same roof as that man is utterly wasted on you." Tess expelled a breath, looking peeved. Well, as peeved as anyone with freckles and a perpetual smile could. "I don't get it, Lor. I've seen the two of you together and deny it all you want, y'all have the hots for each other."

"I don't deny there's an attraction." Although she wondered if it had faded on Sam's part. Whenever their paths had crossed during the past forty-eight hours, he'd seemed prickly, strangely aloof after their former bantering. "But this is not what I wanted to discuss with you. Are you free tonight?"

Tess brightened. "I don't suppose you're asking because you want to set *me* up with Sam?"

"No." Lorelei took care to enunciate the word as forcefully as possible.

"Well, then yes. I'm very disappointed, but I'm also free."

Chapter Twelve

As soon as Sam helped the little girl atop the saddled pony, she began whooping and swinging her cowgirl hat in the air. "Yahoo! Giddyap, pony."

Most of the parents he'd seen today would start snapping pictures now, taking advantage of the pony's steady plodding gait to get some great "action" shots. But the mother and father of the towheaded child who'd introduced herself as Molly were too fixated on each other. The woman was standing with her hands on her hips, talking in a low, clipped voice. Sam couldn't make out any of her words, but the tone was unmistakable. Her husband was equally angry; he kept interrupting, gesturing wildly as he spoke. Damn shame, considering the beautiful day, the jovial surroundings and the fact that their adorable daughter was enjoying a ride on one of the sweetest-natured ponies Sam had ever known.

Yet even in the midst of a sunny Texas afternoon filled with the promise of spring, these two radiated stress and hostility. Practically anything could have set them off. Perhaps the man objected to how much money was being spent on food and festival tchotchkes or maybe the woman was concerned about how much beer he'd imbibed and wanted him to cut back on his refills. Or either one of them could be miffed that his or her spouse had spoken to flirtatiously to someone in the crowd.

A billion things that could go wrong, in Sam's opinion. And sometimes it was no discernible thing at all. When he'd asked Grace Torres one day how she was holding up, mostly just intending to ask after the restaurant business, she'd taken the opportunity to vent her frustration over her brother's separation from his wife.

"I just don't understand!" Grace had railed.

"They love each other so much. Whatever else happened should be secondary to that, right?"

Lots of things in life "should" be, but weren't.

He conjured a smile for the little girl. "Sorry, darlin', your time's up." He helped her slide her feet from the stirrups and walked her back to her bickering parents. The mother took the girl's hand and stalked off, followed closely by the father, whose volume was increasing with each passing word.

"Cute kid. I especially liked her hot pink cowgirl boots," Lorelei observed from his left. "Wonder if they make those in my size."

Sam gave her a weary smile of greeting over his shoulder. "Hey."

"Wow." She took a step closer, squinting up at him. "That bad, huh?"

He shrugged. "Long day. I enjoy the festival, but I'm ready for it to end after about day three. I'm getting restless."

"Ready to leave town?" she asked.

Ready to do just about anything that didn't involve going "home" to her each night. It seemed as if she'd infested every corner of the inn in countless maddening ways. Her scent lingered in rooms long after she'd passed through, teasing him. The sight of a rosy lipstick ring on a tumbler in the sink had made him think about her mouth—more specifically, about kissing her. Even Oberon, the tiny traitor, had abandoned sleeping at the foot of Sam's bed in favor of curling up with Lorelei. *Cat's no fool.*

"What do you want, Lorelei?"

She scowled. "Have I done something to upset you?"

"I'm not upset, just busy."

She turned her head to the left, then to the right in exaggerated slow motion. "You mean because of this huge line of children waiting for a ride?"

"Things will pick up again after the lunch hour's over," he said defensively.

"Tess suggested I find you. We're going out tonight—me, her and Emily Hirsch."

"Are you kidding me? How did Ava recruit you to this groundless cause?" He hadn't been too surprised when Ava had gone out of her way to introduce him to her niece. At least once every three or four months, either Wanda had suggested the name of some nice girl he should take out, or she'd put one of her friends up to the task. But he'd thought that Lorelei had understood his position, that he emphatically was not looking for any serious romantic entanglements. Timid Emily was far too sweet a kid for him to lead on when he had less than zero interest in her.

"Take a breath," Lorelei ordered. "You looked like you were about to reach for your six-shooter and riddle me with bullets. Ava's already apologized for throwing her niece at you. Trust me, Em's not interested. Tess and I just wanted to do something nice by taking her out on her last night in town. And Tess suggested you come along."

"Why?" he asked suspiciously, still apprehensive about a feminine plot.

Lorelei rolled her eyes. "Must be because we wanted the privilege of your gallant and delightful company."

He grated out a laugh. "I did warn you it had been a long day and that I'm cranky."

She regarded him for a long moment, her lips twitching. "You never said anything about cranky."

"It was implied."

"Look, you've been working long hours at the festival and talking to lots of tourists all day. That can be draining."

She was right. Even though he mostly enjoyed interacting with the people who came to the festival, the smiling alone made his face hurt by the end of the day, to say nothing of the small talk. How in the hell did politicians do it?

"You could probably use some fun tonight," she continued. "Unwind, recharge your batteries. And Tess and Ava both live in the opposite direction of the bar than the inn. If I can ride back with *you* instead of asking Tess or Emily..."

"Which bar did you guys pick?" If she thought she could talk him into line-dancing, she didn't know him at all.

She rattled off the name of one of the local places with no dance floor. "Thought we'd keep it low-key. Tess says tonight is trivia night. We can play on teams."

He wasn't sure that he wanted to go, but at least he'd be away from the inn and the dozen distractions that were Lorelei. If they were out in public, he had a better chance of keeping his hands off of her. *Maybe*. "And you're sure I won't be intruding on girls' night?"

"We'd like it if you joined us." She bit her lip, looking vulnerable, and he regretted how surly he'd been. "*I'd* like it."

He nodded sharply. "Just tell me what time to be ready."

Sam hadn't said much on the ride from the B and B to the tavern. Lorelei wondered if she'd done the right thing, letting Tess talk her into bringing Sam.

"You swear this has nothing to do with your thinking I should make a move on Sam?" Lorelei had asked one last time before she'd tracked him down at the festival.

"I swear," Tess had vowed. "If I had any ulterior motives, it would be about *me* getting a love life. Guys are more likely to approach us if we have a man around." Her theory had been "too intimidating if it's all chicks. But mostly, I just think it would be fun if Sam joins us."

Stealing a glance at his profile in the cab of the truck, Lorelei thought "fun" might be too high an expectation. She was disconcerted by his mood. For a few days, he'd been so playful that she'd almost forgotten his taciturn side, but it had returned with a vengeance. *Pity.* With her leaving soon, this wasn't how she wanted to remember him. But it was probably for the best that she saw him with no illusions.

By the time they got to the bar, Emily and Tess had already been seated at a U-shaped booth. The four of them ordered sodas and an assortment of appetizers for the table to share. A man with a microphone introduced himself as Andy Schubert and explained that in a few minutes, they would get started with T.E.X.A.S. trivia. All questions fell into the categories of Today (pop culture and modern life), Entertainment, "X-tra" Credit (really tough questions to help separate the average from the champions), Ancient/Not-So-Ancient History and Sports. Waitresses were circulating with pencils and slips of paper for answers.

"So you guys put together your teams," Andy announced, "and get ready to battle for our great prizes, generously donated by local sponsors."

After the man was finished recognizing the sponsors, Sam unfolded his long legs and he rose from the booth. "I'll let you ladies decide on the team name. I'm going to say hi to Andy."

Tess plunked a tortilla chip into the spicy, black-bean-based "cowboy caviar." "I don't care what we call ourselves as long as we win," she said merrily. "The gift certificates are all for places in town and since I'm the only one who truly lives here, I figure I get to keep them."

Lorelei laughed. "So basically, we're just your minions, here to—"

"Lorelei Keller?" A dark-haired man in slacks and a white button-down shirt stopped next to them, smiling down at her with warm familiarity. And he was smiling down from quite a height. The tall stranger had at least a few extra inches on Sam.

I should know who he is, shouldn't I? Drat. She quickly skimmed through her memory bank. Honestly, you'd think someone around six-five would stand out.

Across the table, Tess saved her. "Brody! I don't think I've seen you since high school."

Right. The name clicked into place. Brody Jenkins.

"It has been a while," Brody agreed. "I'm with an engineering firm in Austin now, but I came to town for the festival. I just completed a hellacious project at work and thought I needed a few days off, so I came to stay with my parents."

"Good to see you," Tess said. "This is our friend Emily, from San Marcos, and of course you remember Lorelei."

His hazel eyes returned to Lorelei's face. "How could I forget? You're the one who got away."

That announcement startled her. "I am?"

He grinned. "I meant to ask you out all

through high school, but I was busy with basketball. And possibly a little daunted," he admitted. "You were one of the only students who could beat my scores on math exams."

She smiled but was distracted from answering by Sam's scowl. He'd returned to the table and stood impatiently behind Brody.

"Oh, sorry, man." Brody followed her gaze and stepped aside. "Am I in the way?"

"This is Sam Travis." Lorelei made the introductions as Sam reclaimed his seat next to her. "Sam, Brody Jenkins. He went to school with Tess and me."

Tess turned her head, looking around the room. "Are you here with someone, Brody?"

He shrugged. "I met a buddy for a beer, but he just left. Newly married, didn't want to be out late. They're still in that honeymoon phase." His gaze flickered from Sam back to Lorelei, specifically to her left hand. "Are you two...?"

"Ha! Not at all," Lorelei said.

She knew from the way Sam stiffened next to her and Tess's quizzical look that her denial had been a bit too resounding. But really, the idea of Sam Travis doing something as crazy as getting engaged or, heaven forbid, getting married? *It is to laugh.*

"You should join us," Tess invited. She beamed. "Yet another person who doesn't live here who can slave for me. My diabolical plan is to surround myself with people who can answer the questions, then selfishly reap the rewards. You're smart, right? Went to UT on scholarship?"

"Basketball scholarship," he clarified. "But I held my own on the dean's list."

"Awesome, you're hired. Scooch over," Tess instructed Emily. The quiet blonde slid farther toward the middle, leaving room for Brody on the end, directly across from Lorelei.

Tess turned to Emily with a suddenly stern look. "Wait, I didn't check your credentials. You're smart enough to win me prizes, right?"

"Salutatorian in high school. But it was a graduating class of like fifty," the woman added with a modest grin. "So I'm not sure that counts."

"Good enough for my purposes," Tess declared. "I think our team name should be Empress and the Minions. Hey, it's better than Three Chicks and Two Dudes."

"Only marginally," Lorelei said.

Andy tapped on his microphone and announced they were getting started, lobbing out an "easy" question to get the crowd warmed up. It was about an award-winning actor and Emily announced in an excited whisper, "I know this one!" before Andy had even finished reading from his card. A few minutes later, Lorelei found herself thinking that they should have taken Emily out for trivia days ago. Knowing half the answers was obviously good for her confidence, and it allowed her to interact with others without struggling for appropriate personal conversation.

Emily's increasingly bright smile was a nice counterpoint to the dark thundercloud over Sam's head. *Inviting him was a mistake.* He'd barely said two sentences since he'd come back to the table and found Brody chatting with Lorelei. And Sam remained stonily silent through most of the questions. Because he didn't know the answers or because he didn't want to be here?

When Andy announced that one of the extra credit questions, worth two points, was a math problem, half the people in the bar groaned.

Brody, however, rubbed his hands in glee, grinning across the table at Lorelei. "We got this one, Ivy League."

At the end of the first round, answer sheets

had to be turned in at the bar so standings could be calculated. And, the owners hoped, so that people had a good window of opportunity to spend more money on drinks and food.

Sam grabbed the piece of paper Tess had been using to record answers. "I'll take it up there. Might as well contribute something, right?"

Lorelei's heart squeezed. She couldn't help watching his progress to the bar, her attention only half on Brody as he talked to her.

"So how often do you get down here?" he asked. They'd established earlier that she'd remained in Pennsylvania after college.

"Almost never," she said absently. "But I've really been enjoying this trip." She caught herself and shook her head at the bizarre statement. "Well, not the part where I had to say goodbye to my mom! But…"

"We knew what you meant," Tess assured her. "And you know Wanda would have wanted you to enjoy your visit. She loved the festival."

Lorelei nodded. "If you guys will excuse me? I think I'm gonna run to the ladies' room before we start the next round." She swept up her purse but instead of heading for the restrooms in the far corner, she detoured through the center of the room, pulled toward Sam as if by a giant, unseen magnet.

He doesn't need a magnet to draw women to him. Not when he has those eyes.

He'd already turned back toward the table and they almost collided. "Sorry, didn't realize you were behind me," he said.

"I wanted to talk to you. Away from the others. You're not having any fun, are you?"

"Is that your polite way of saying I'm raining on everyone else's parade?" He shoved a hand through his hair. "I shouldn't have come. If I cut out early, do you think..." He glared in the direction of their table. "I'll bet Jenkins would be happy to give you a ride."

Beneath his brusque demeanor, some emotion had glimmered in Sam's expression. *Jealousy?* Lorelei was dimly ashamed of how happy that possibility made her. She couldn't help herself, though. The idea that Sam might want her felt really, really good.

Because I want him.

No matter what she'd told Tess or what logical reminders she gave herself, her unwise attraction to Sam had only grown this week, not diminished. And the idea of him leaving her here tonight, when they had so little time left together anyway…

She put a hand on his arm. "Actually, I think calling it a night might be a good idea. This place is a little too crowded for me." She cast a glance back at their table, where Tess and Emily were both giggling at something Brody had said.

Sam's expression was pained. "You don't have to humor me. You should stay with them, enjoy yourself."

"But…" She stopped and took a steadying breath. *Just do it.*

What did she have to lose? She and Sam were going to part ways soon so even if she abjectly humiliated herself in the next sixty seconds, it's not as though it would have any bearing on the rest of her life. Except, of course, for the deep and painful emotional scars, she thought wryly. The words she wanted to say were risky—even knowing he had some physical attraction to her, she couldn't know whether he'd reject her.

He'd stilled, his body thrumming with a new tension she could practically *hear,* like the electricity currents running through power lines. He studied her with those green eyes that seemed to see more of her than anyone else had before. "But what, Lorelei?"

"I don't want to stay and 'enjoy myself.' I'd rather go back to the inn. And enjoy you." The daring announcement might have been more effective if it hadn't been delivered in a whisper.

Then again, maybe not. Judging from the way Sam sucked in his breath, her words had definitely had an effect.

"Lorelei." Her name came out as a groan. And it had never sounded sexier. "You don't belong with me. You deserve someone like him." Sam jerked his chin in Brody's general direction but never took his eyes off of her.

Warmth unfurled inside her. That was his argument? Not a reminder that he wasn't looking for any romantic complications in his life, just "you deserve..." Didn't every woman deserve, at least once in her life, to be with a man who made her body tingle and her pulse race? A man who could make her forget how to breathe with his incomparable kisses?

Emboldened, she took a step closer. "I know you don't want a girlfriend. But do you want me? I'll be gone soon, but for now... Let's look at it as my being on vacation. Would a vacation fling really be so bad, something for us both to remember fondly after the inn is sold and we've both moved on from here?" He would come back, she was sure, but he'd made it clear that he wouldn't put down roots.

His dazed eyes were locked on her mouth and he was breathing more heavily. But he was obviously conflicted. "You just lost a parent. That's enough to leave anyone emotionally vulnerable. I won't take advantage of you," he said raggedly.

She grabbed hold of his black T-shirt, the cotton soft in her hands. "This isn't about my being needy or being afraid to be alone, I swear. I can't stop thinking about what it would be like. I've been—"

The rest of her words were lost in his kiss. His mouth crushed hers, the intensity of his embrace proving that she hadn't been the only one thinking about them together. Her fingers tightened on his shirt, and she arched into him, kissing him back for all she was worth.

"You have *got* to be kidding me!" Barbara Biggins made a derisive, unladylike harrumphing noise. "Will you two just get a freaking room already?"

Sam met Lorelei's gaze, his words for her ears only. "Sounds like a good idea to me."

* * *

As Lorelei fiddled with the truck's radio dial, Sam made a concerted effort not to floor the accelerator. A speeding ticket would delay their getting back to the inn. And his getting Lorelei into bed.

His heart thumped in an irregular pattern as he tried to process what awaited him. For the past three days, it seemed as if he'd been fantasizing about her constantly. It was difficult to believe those fantasies were finally going to come true.

She wants me? Didn't she know she could do better than a cowboy with calloused hands and a couple of semesters of community college? With women like Barbara, he could understand the pursuit. It wasn't about him as an individual, it was about the hunt. He'd garnered a reputation for being aloof; breaking through that would mean a woman had *won.* Even though he'd continue freely roaming the streets instead of having his head mounted on a wall, he'd still be little more than a trophy.

But Lorelei hadn't been pursuing him. She'd spent her first few days in town snapping at him. And if she'd wanted to seduce him, she wouldn't have passed up a golden opportunity like the other night. When he'd turned the corner and found her dripping wet, with only a piece of terry cloth keeping her naked body from his sight… Sam's fingers tightened on the steering wheel and he shifted uncomfortably, his jeans no longer the relaxed fit they'd been an hour ago.

Say something. Making conversation might help distract him long enough to get blood to his brain. And talking to her seemed like the gentlemanly thing to do. It would be creepy to drive in silence for ten minutes, then pounce on her the minute they set foot in the B and B.

"So, uh…" He cleared his throat. "They were pretty understanding about our bailing on the team."

They must have witnessed his and Lorelei's kiss from the horseshoe-shaped booth. Emily had been gaping at them and Tess had been grinning from ear to ear. Sam had studiously avoided glancing toward Jenkins; he'd worried he wouldn't be able to keep the smugness out of his expression and Lorelei was more than some conquest to gloat over.

"Understanding?" Lorelei echoed. "Tess chased us away so fast you'd think she owed us money."

True. The redhead had no semblance of a poker face. For a moment, he'd actually thought she was going to admonish them to have fun but not to forget to use condoms. He frowned. It had been a while—did he *have* condoms? *Nightstand.* Thank goodness.

In his peripheral vision, he noticed how lights from outside glinted off the jet buttons on her dress. The casual outfit—which stopped a couple of inches above her knees, hardly revealing—had been driving him nuts all night. In a bar of women wearing tight jeans and a few low-cut tops, he'd been obsessed with a flowing black dress with loose, elbow-length sleeves. Probably because it buttoned from just below the vee neckline straight down to the hem. He hadn't been able to look at her once without thinking about *un*buttoning. A few quick movements of nimble fingers, and she'd be—

Lorelei leaned forward again and resumed messing with the radio stations.

"Can't find any songs you like?" he asked.

"Nervous energy," she confessed. "Guess I'm just looking for something to keep my hands occupied."

He had several suggestions. None of which were appropriate while he was operating a motor vehicle. By "nervous," he hoped she didn't mean she regretted her impulsive words at the bar. How did he let her know he understood if she changed her mind without making it sound as if he didn't want her? Because he couldn't recall wanting a woman this badly before.

Moments later, they drove behind the inn. Sam squeezed the steering wheel. "You're still good with this? I mean, if you were just caught up in the moment earlier…"

She gave him a dumbfounded look. "Caught up in the moment? Sam, when I propositioned you, we were in the middle of a trivia game and you were stomping around like a grouchy bear. With that backdrop, you're worried I was so overcome with lust that I talked myself into something I'll regret?"

"When you put it like that…" He unfastened his seat belt and reached for her, pulling her closer on the bench seat. She seemed startled but came into his arms.

"You know, there are some comfy beds inside," she teased, even as she tilted her face up for a kiss.

He was stalling out here because it was too tempting to rush her into one of those beds. Sam had been around enough of the local vintners to hear lots of commentary on properly tasting wine. Talk of "bouquets" and "citrus tones" and "complexity" had always sounded a little pretentious to him. But after tonight, he might have a better appreciation for a slow, measured sensory approach because he truly wanted to savor Lorelei. He wanted to breathe her in and let her taste linger on his tongue. He wanted to close his eyes and lose himself in her.

Threading his fingers through her hair, he kissed her thoroughly, deeply, but he didn't hurry, letting the need build for both of them. She began wriggling in an unsuccessful attempt to get closer and making *mmm* sounds that were somewhere between a whimper and sigh. The only flaw in Sam's plan to kiss her out in the truck and stoke the desire between them? In order to get inside, they would have to *stop.* He couldn't bring himself to, not yet.

He did move away from her mouth, though, sketching quick light kisses along her jaw before moving to the soft skin of her neck. When he nipped slightly just below her ear, she rewarded him with a low moan that had him as hard as a rock. He rubbed a thumb over her collarbone, then traced a deliberate line down into her cleavage before cupping a breast through the satiny fabric of her dress. She arched against his palm and Sam fumbled behind him for the door handle. As they slid out of the truck, he realized his truck windows were fogged up, as if they'd been a couple of high school kids parking. Not that Lorelei would ever have gone out with him when they were teenagers—they would have had nothing in common, and he suspected she'd been too busy trying to get into the right college.

Well, we're adults now. And tonight she was his.

Holding her tucked in the crook of his arm, as if he couldn't bear any distance between them, he steered them toward the door. They were already kissing again by the time the cat met them in the kitchen, meowing at them like some incensed chaperone, as if to say, *And* just what do *you think you two are doing?*

"My room?" Sam asked.

"Fine with me," she murmured, her eyes glazed with need.

At the top of the stairs, he scooped her up. Her arm went around his neck and she nuzzled his chest.

"Don't distract me or you might get dropped," he warned. Did she have any idea how good she felt against him?

He kicked the door shut behind them and righted her at the foot of the bed. He bent his head to kiss her but missed. She'd already dropped into a sitting position on the edge of the mattress. Looking up at him through her lashes, she reached for the top button of her dress. His mouth went dry.

"I like that dress," he said. "Do you know it has exactly nine buttons? I counted."

Her lips curved in a slow grin. "So that's why I felt your eyes on me tonight, purely numerical interest?" She slid the first button free, then the second. By the time she reached the third, he realized it was a good thing *she* was unfastening them. His hands felt shaky.

Luckily, his own shirt was simple to remove. He whipped it over his head, then reached for her, raising her to her feet with only half of the buttons undone. He tucked his fingers inside the gaping panels of fabric and shoved lightly. The material whispered down her body and pooled at her feet. She stood before him in sandals and a matching set of a black bra and panties. The lingerie was simple, but curves like hers didn't need any extra embellishment to be mind-numbingly erotic.

"Lorelei." It felt like a prayer on his lips. He reached for her, kissing her hungrily. His hands were just as greedy, wanting to touch every inch of her warm skin. He skimmed over her back, down the graceful length of her spine to cup her butt, holding her closer as he rocked his hips into hers.

She raked her fingernails across his chest, then toward the denim waistband of his jeans. His entire body tensed in anticipation. Finally, she brushed over his erection and Sam hissed a breath through grated teeth.

"Gotta get out of these jeans," he said.

Instead of helping him, she kicked off her shoes and reclined across the bed, watching avidly. Seeing how clearly she desired him was nearly as powerful a turn-on as her touch had been.

Stripped down to a pair of boxer briefs, he joined her on the bed. He drank in the sight of her then surprised them both by almost laughing.

She propped herself up on an elbow. "What's funny?"

"You remember that day you went to the wine tastings? I came back and you were lying across the couch?" Her relaxed body had seemed so pliant and welcoming, her smile when she'd seen him so unrestrained.

"At the time, I wondered what could possibly be sexier. But this is way better."

She ducked her gaze for a moment, incongruently shy after she'd shucked her clothes. "I'd been thinking of you all that afternoon. I could blame the wine, but..."

"You remind me of wine." He gently pushed her onto her back.

She narrowed her eyes. "Say 'full-bodied' and die."

He ignored the crazy talk—her body was perfect—and kissed her neck. "You smell good," he murmured against her skin. Like honeysuckle, only naughtier. "I detect floral notes," he deadpanned.

She chuckled but the amusement in her eyes dissolved into heat when he reached for the front clasp of her bra. He ran his thumb over the swell of her breast. "Pale, perfect color." In ever narrowing circles, he swept his finger around her puckered nipple, listening to her breathing grow more frantic. He leaned over her breast, not touching but close enough that she could feel his breath. "And these remind me of berries. Exotic and—" he scraped his tongue over her "—delicious."

She writhed and Sam drew her into his mouth, lost. He'd wanted to woo her, but he had no words left now, only a need to touch her, to be inside her. By the time he eventually sheathed himself in a condom and thrust into the slickness of her, the only word he knew was her name.

Lorelei woke up slowly as if she didn't want to leave a particularly pleasant dream. She was exhausted and could tell even before she opened her eyes that it was still dark. Moonlight peeked through the blinds on the window, falling across Sam's face. He looked utterly at peace and she grinned, glad to have done her part in relaxing him.

When she tried to slide out from under his arm he made a small noise of protest and snuggled her closer into his bare chest. If she weren't so thirsty, she probably could have happily stayed there for hours—days—on end. Come to think of it, though, she was hungry, too. Neither of them had eaten much at the bar and they'd left early. She should treat herself to something down in the kitchen—heaven knew they'd worked off some calories. They'd made love twice before falling asleep.

He'd surprised her in bed. Monosyllable Man could be poetic when he was duly inspired. Also, for a man who seemed so intent on keeping control of his life—by keeping others at a distance—he'd had no trouble at all ceding control to her when they'd had sex. The second time, she'd wanted to set the pace. She'd explored his taut body before straddling him and guiding him into her.

She bit her lip at the memory, thinking that if she didn't hurry up and get out of this bed, she might not make it down to the kitchen for something to eat after all. Stepping over their discarded clothes, she headed into the bathroom and grabbed the robe off the brass hook. When she came back into the bedroom, Sam was gone.

Like minds? She wondered. He had to have worked up an appetite, too.

Downstairs, she found him pulling containers out of the refrigerator. She stopped in the doorway to admire the view of his ass in the form-fitting gray boxer briefs. Maybe food could wait after all.

His body stilled suddenly; she must have made a noise to give herself away. As he slowly turned toward her, he drawled, "You keep starin', you're gonna bore holes in me."

She laughed. "We've been here before, haven't we?" It seemed like a long time ago, that night she'd come down here for a midnight snack and had ended up arguing with Sam about who should have the inn. Then, she couldn't have imagined wanting to stay in town a day longer than absolutely necessary. And now? She would be sorry to leave.

It wasn't just the green-eyed cowboy and great sex she'd miss—although, right now, those topped the list. She was also enjoying the people and the food and the pace. Though she'd always claimed to love her job, she hadn't realized how much it could drain her—the long hours, the stressing over whether a project was absolutely perfect, whether it would be enough to help her move ahead.

That's it, she decided in a flash of insight. As far back as she could remember, her life had been about moving. Moving past her dad's death, moving out of Texas to go to school, moving to the top of her classes in college, moving ahead at work…

When was the last time she'd simply stood still and enjoyed where she was? Savored the moment?

"Lorelei?" He'd set the food on the counter and was studying her with naked curiosity. "You still with me?"

"I'm here." *Here and now. And happy.* But two in the morning didn't seem like the time to share the revelation she'd just had. Besides, they'd been having a spectacular night. If she told him that suddenly she wasn't so eager to return to life in Philly, he might worry that she'd recanted her "fling" philosophy and was looking for something more permanent. "I was just thinking about that night we ran into each other in the kitchen and you offered me cake."

He came toward her, his expression wicked in the shadows. "That reminds me. There was something I wanted to do that night." He kept walking and didn't stop when he reached her, instead backing her into the wall without actually touching her.

Lorelei licked her lips, her heart thudding faster. "Yeah? What's that?"

In answer, he reached for both her hands, raising them over her head and holding them against the wall. When he kissed her, her body went so liquid she wouldn't have been able to stand without his support.

Food would *definitely* have to wait.

Chapter Thirteen

Lorelei was glad this trail ride was only a two-day event. She hadn't brought many pairs of jeans with her. Sam had grunted his approval when he saw her bag that she knew how to "pack light." Truthfully, it wasn't as though she'd had that many options.

He was outside putting their stuff in the bed of the truck and she was taking the quiet moment alone to regroup. When they came back, this would all be over. Sam had other jobs lined up, other places to be, and the real estate company would begin showing the inn to potential buyers. Even though Lorelei would be back here after the campout, this felt like goodbye.

She looked around the sun-filled kitchen, memories swirling together. While she and her mother might have had their differences, Wanda had loved her and had tried to make her trips home fun-filled. She remembered three Christmases ago, when her mother had finally coerced her into sharing some spiked eggnog, and they'd attempted to build a gingerbread house together. They'd giggled at the "structurally unsound" results while licking frosting off their fingers.

"No way would any company ever allow home-owners insurance on this wreck," Lorelei had said on a laugh.

More recently, Lorelei had joked with Ava and Tess in this same kitchen. And, night before last, made love with Sam. Heat blazed into her cheeks as she recalled the intensity with which he'd taken her against the wall. Even if she hadn't wanted to run this place, and certainly couldn't envision herself organizing ghost tours year-round, she felt a fondness toward the inn she'd never experienced before.

"You were right, Mom," she whispered. "I'm glad I came for the festival." Lorelei almost laughed when she heard the soft tinkling of the dragonfly chimes, even though she knew it was simply the breeze through the window, not a reply from the Great Beyond.

Wait. Didn't Ava have those chimes now? She whipped her head around to glare at the empty hook over the kitchen sink.

"Knock knock?" The back door swung open and Ava stepped inside. "I just came to tell you guys to have a nice trip and promise that I'll actually interact with Oberon. Even if I have to wear gloves and football pads to protect myself."

Lorelei laughed. "Believe it or not, he seems like he's mellowed. Sam and I both pet him on a near daily basis and still have ten fingers each." Of course, the cat had been furious when they'd locked him out of Sam's room again last night. She frowned suddenly, making a mental note to close her and Sam's bedroom doors before they left. Just in case Obie objected to being left behind.

"I also wanted to stop by before you left to make sure you were feeling okay. Emily mentioned that you and Sam left rather abruptly the other night?" Ava raised her glance to the ceiling, not meeting Lorelei's eyes. "And no one's seen either of you since."

Though it was obvious by Ava's forced nonchalance that she'd already deduced what happened, Lorelei couldn't bring herself to acknowledge it. "What do you mean no one's seen us?" She did her best to sound mystified. "We've been around. Just, um, a little busy getting ready for the trail ride."

"Uh-huh."

Lorelei was utterly grateful when Sam came inside, putting a damper on Ava's questions.

"All ready?" Sam asked. Lorelei nodded and they both said goodbye to Ava.

They were several miles down the road before she realized she'd forgotten to close the bedroom doors. Oh, well. If the cat was moved to show his displeasure over their being gone, it wasn't as if there weren't targets all through the inn.

"Hey, Sam? I've been thinking about Oberon. What are we going to do with him? Mom mentioned that the inn is his home, but neither of us are staying. And I don't think Ava's bonded with him quite like we have."

"So what do you suggest, some kind of split custody arrangement? You take him year-round and he can stay with me for the summer and Christmas break?"

"Ha-ha. I was being serious."

He hesitated. "You know I'm not very stationary. I have my trailer, but he's used to a lot more room. Plus, there are coyotes nearby and if he were ever to get out… I, uh, I've gotten kind of used to the little bugger. I didn't mean to, but it'll be tough to see him go." Braking at a red light, Sam turned to capture her gaze with his. "Probably best for me not to hold on, though."

The backs of her eyes burned. So did her throat, making it difficult to speak. Then the light turned green, Sam looked away and the moment passed.

A few minutes later, when the silence felt oppressive, she said, "I guess I'll take him, then." It came out sounding resentful, which she didn't mean. She'd grown accustomed to having the cat around, too. Seeing his fuzzy face when she came through the door after a long day would make her feel a lot less lonely back in Philadelphia.

"You sure you don't mind?" Sam asked. "I recall your saying something once about not being cut out to own pets."

"Yeah." She stared out the window. "But I've…changed since I got here." *In more ways than you want to know about.*

Owning a cat was the least of her worries.

* * *

Sam's eyebrows were raised as he took in Lorelei's fretful expression. Keeping his voice low enough that none of the tourists or ranch hands in the long barn overheard, he whispered, "You told me you liked horses, that you've been riding before."

"I have. Maybe it's been even longer than I realized, but… I'm good with the horses."

He leaned in close enough that he could smell her shampoo beneath the sweet, earthy scent of hay. "Then what's the problem? You looked upset."

She sighed. "I was just analyzing all the things that could go wrong on a trail ride like this! Bad habit, I know. But do you have any idea the kind of *liability*—"

He laughed then, barely resisting the urge kiss her. So she was worried not as an equestrienne, but as an actuary? "Everyone's signed their waivers, darlin'. And we'll be careful, I promise."

On the hour long drive to the ranch, she'd explained to him in detail what she did for a living. *Still don't get it.* But he understood the gist, which was good enough. Especially since she was leaving in the next couple of days. It wasn't as if there were going to be a pop quiz.

Now, if he had to pass a test on the exact shade of Lorelei's eyes or the gamut of sounds she made as she approached an orgasm, he knew he could ace it.

He gave himself a mental shake. A distracted trail boss was no way to prevent those accidents she feared.

The ranch and horses were owned by a family who'd hired Sam for a variety of odd jobs in the past. The family's patriarch was approaching seventy now and no longer did the overnight trips. His son headed them up frequently but a couple of years ago, when his wife had been going through a difficult pregnancy, he'd entrusted a group to Sam. Since then, Sam did several a year so that the man wouldn't have to be away from his spouse and two young children so often.

"I know it's just for the night, but you'll understand when you have kids of your own. At this age, it's too easy to miss a first smile, first word, first step."

All milestones Sam had no intention of ever experiencing, but he hadn't wanted to sound like a child-hating cynic. The truth was, he was fond of kids. In the generic sense.

Some of the trail rides he worked were specifically geared toward young riders—just not this one, with its spooky stories this evening and bat expedition. This ride was only for eighteen and up, but he couldn't help grinning inwardly at how panicked Lorelei would be if children, with all the potential mishaps they could cause, were added to the mix.

Kids were fun. As long as he didn't have to parent them. He wasn't sure any of the male role models in his life had been helpful. There was his biological father who'd worked himself into an early grave; Lorelei's father had also died young, but at least he hadn't ignored his only child her entire life. And his stepfather was a shallow, superficial man who cared more about appearances than family bonds. Even JD was a questionable influence. The womanizing bachelor had only had relationships that lasted from Friday night until Monday morning.

If Sam had seen more evidence of how to make a relationship work, how to balance the responsibility of providing with the joys of being together, would he be less wary of relationships now? Would he be able to let himself fall in love?

His gaze skittered back to Lorelei and he

rubbed his chest. Something that felt like heartburn hampered his breathing for a second, but then he walked away from her, telling himself he had a job to do. The eleven tourists gathered needed to get acquainted with their mounts. Standing here and playing what-if wasn't going to accomplish anything.

By four o'clock that afternoon, Lorelei was really having to bite her tongue to keep from whining, "Are we there yet?"

No one else was complaining. Then again, she was probably the only person who'd spent the thirty-six hours prior to climbing into the saddle having energetic sex. There had been a brief period this afternoon when she'd been only pleasantly sore. The rolling gait of the horse beneath her had simply made her aware of the places she still tingled from Sam's touch.

But now there was no "pleasantly" about it. *Ow, dammit.* All she wanted was to throw herself from the mare's back, catch a cab—which seemed unlikely out here in the middle of nowhere—and get back to the inn, where she could soak in the tub with some mineral salts for her sore muscles. She didn't even care if Oberon came into the bathroom to keep her company. Hell, he could swim around in the tub as long as he left her alone to whimper in peace.

When Sam announced that they'd reached the spot where they'd be making camp for the evening, she could have kissed him. Except, probably not, because that proved to lead to other things and her body ached far too much to even contemplate that.

People began dismounting. The chuck-wagon cook and the rider Sam was training to be an eventual trail boss himself were helping to secure the horses.

Sam came over to assist Lorelei. As much as she'd been looking forward to getting down off her horse, she found that she had to do so very gingerly.

"You okay?" To his credit, Sam tried to sound and look concerned. But other emotions were seeping into his expression—knowing amusement and sizzling desire, as he obviously recalled how she'd come to be sore in the first place and how much he'd like to do that again.

"Not gonna happen," she growled.

"I don't know what you're talking about," he said innocently. Then he gave her an evil grin. "'Course, if what you meant was that

I have to keep my hands to myself, it's only fair to let you know that I have some really great cream to rub on sore muscles. And I had planned to offer to massage it in personally."

"You're supposed to be solicitous of the riders under your care, not looking for ways to get them out of their jeans," she scolded. "Are all trail bosses this one-track-minded?"

"When they have a woman who looks like you to share their tent? Absolutely."

Despite pretending to be appalled by his ulterior motives, she had to admit his desire wasn't one-sided. Seeing Sam out here, clearly in his element, was incredibly sexy. All through the day, he'd shared historical anecdotes, such as the Texas "camel experiment" in the mid-1800s and the Mason County Hoodoo War. If their trivia game the other night had included any questions about Texas government, the Civil War, Native American tribes from this region, livestock or weather phenomena, Sam would have cleaned house. He had an easy confidence in the saddle and seemed to truly love the land he was showing them.

And Ava had been right. He was definitely a natural-born storyteller. He'd led them through a narrow pass earlier that day and told them in quiet, somber tones that had somehow carried down the line of riders that the area was reputed to be haunted by a brokenhearted woman who'd been betrayed by her family.

"She fell in love with a Chanas brave and planned to sneak away from her family in the night to join his nomadic tribe. But her brother caught her and her father, in a rage, shoved her from that peak, declaring that he'd rather see his daughter dead than turn her back on who she was. It's said that when her father realized what he'd done, he shot himself and that both her uneasy spirit and his remain here, never able to find peace with each other. Their ongoing anger is the explanation for many strange happenings."

With Sam as their leader, Lorelei didn't think twice about what kind of bugs might be buzzing about their tents tonight or the seasonal allergies that sometimes plagued her when the weather turned warm. He was mesmerizing.

The group was instructed to set up tents while it was still plenty bright outside. Then they were going to take two hiking excursions while the camp cook fixed dinner—the first to a nearby natural cavern, the second to see a bat colony.

"It's still a bit early in the year, but they do start returning to the area in March," Sam told them. "So cross your fingers."

He took time assisting everyone, checking the horses' shoes with a middle-aged man who was a Houston stockbroker in his real life "but always wanted to be a cowboy." Then he helped a woman taking this family trip with her two college-age daughters pitch their tent. A man and wife in their early sixties were obviously veteran campers; the couple didn't need technical support so much as they needed a good-natured referee for their squabbling. Otherwise, they'd never finish setting up before dark. Finally, Sam came over to inspect the job Lorelei was doing.

"Tent looks good, Ms. Keller. Nice job," he praised. "Which is important. Because it would be *such* a shame if this collapsed in the middle of the night and you had to bunk with someone else." The look he gave her tent left her half alarmed that he planned to sabotage the stakes as soon as her back was turned.

"A male someone," he added. "You know, to protect you from beasties. Wolves, javelinas. The occasional *El Chupacabra.*"

"Bunk with a man? What kind of example would that set for those college girls?" she chided lightly. How far into the night would it be before she caved to the temptation of snuggling into Sam's sleeping bag with him?

"Right, because being college girls, they've probably never heard about sex," he scoffed.

"Well, they didn't hear about it from *me.*"

He laughed. "Such a virtuous and pure-hearted woman. Must be why I love you."

Lorelei was highly intelligent; she knew he was kidding and meant nothing by the words, knew it straight to her core. Yet she couldn't prevent the way she trembled inside at the declaration. *Why I love you...*

Worse than her involuntary emotional response, he *saw* her react, if only for a millisecond. Sam's playful mien froze in place like a mask, a caricature of itself.

Oh, please don't. She braced herself for his stilted apology, his polite explanation that he'd only been kidding. That would be too humiliating to endure—not only a rejection, but also his thinking she was so unreasonably deluded she might actually be seeking more from him. If nothing else, she hoped he respected her intellect more than that. She was smart enough to embrace the truth: it would be a monumental mistake to fall for Sam Travis.

That just hadn't stopped her from doing it.

Once again, Lorelei was the outsider. And that campfire revelation stung so badly that she realized she was no longer accustomed to this feeling, could no longer shrug it off. Sometime during her stay in Fredericksburg, she'd started to feel as if she belonged.

Wish I were back in town now.

Around her, the tourists fell into two groups. Those who lounged in that particular boneless lassitude stemming from any active day in the open air, and those who were literally on the edge of their seats—in this case, portable foam mats—tense with expectation as Sam wove another tale. His narratives tonight had begun with a mix of supernatural ghost stories alongside explanations of natural marvels, including a mass of granite that had once terrified superstitious settlers because of the noises it made when the granite contracted in the cool night air and the blue sparks it could generate. As the sun had dipped lower on the horizon and stars began to twinkle overhead, he also pointed out some constellations and threw in some Greek myths for his captive audience.

Lorelei, however, was neither relaxed nor able to lose herself in Sam's baritone. She was seething.

Ever since that awkward moment this afternoon, Sam had been growing more aloof with her. When they'd hiked to a cave after camp was set up, she'd stopped at one point to take in the breathtaking view and Sam had come after her to make sure she wasn't injured or too tired to keep going. She'd reflexively reached for his hand as she told him how beautiful it was here, and he'd stiffened.

"We're holding up the group. We should move on," he'd chastised her mildly. Though his tone hadn't been harsh, it had been far from tender.

He'd been subtly pushing her away for hours now. Apparently, his slip of the tongue had been enough of a reminder for him that this—that *she*—wasn't what he wanted in the long run. Did he think it was kinder this way, to withdraw so that she got angry or that her ego was stung enough she no longer wanted to be with him? Maybe he thought it saved them from a messy goodbye, but all it was doing so far was ticking her off. They were both adults and they'd had an agreement going into this weekend. She would have honored his feelings; there was no need to act like a boyfriend who'd lost interest and was trying to give her the brush-off.

"...but of course, the Germans have lots of legends, too," he was saying. She realized she'd tuned out some Hispanic folklore he'd shared. He had now moved on to other cultures with major influence in the region. "Including a seafaring legend that shares its name with one of our campers." He met her eyes then, raising his cup of water in wry salute.

"There's an 'echoing rock' on the Rhine River called the Lorelei that has been the site of many boating accidents. Skeptics say the murmuring 'voice' associated with the rock comes from a nearby waterfall, while others believe stories of an otherworldly female with a beautiful voice. A siren or mermaid who lures sailors in, bewitching them until they knowingly steer right into their own ruin."

As if a woman by dint of being confident enough to call out to a man and let him know he was wanted was a nefarious enchantress, a threat? *Screw this.* Though Sam's voice was smooth, his expression bland, she heard his words as an indictment. She hadn't been plotting his seduction, hoping to snare him. Frankly, she didn't think *he* was the one who'd been hurt by their short-lived affair. Because you had to let yourself care to be hurt.

Lorelei loudly faked a yawn. "Fascinating stuff. But I'm afraid I'm beat." She stood, trying to look relaxed instead of stalking to her tent. "'Night, everyone."

As soon as she was zipped in for the night, she'd check to see if she had enough bars out here to text Tess and beg her for a ride. If her friend couldn't come pick her up from the ranch tomorrow, Lorelei would devise a Plan B. Because no way in hell was she riding with Sam Travis, spinner of tall tales and emotional coward.

Chapter Fourteen

It was time to go home, back to her real life. Lorelei stood in the driveway of the Haunted Hill Country Bed-and-Breakfast with Ava, who would be driving her to the airport, and Tess, who had come to say goodbye.

Lorelei hugged the redhead whose friendship she'd come to value, especially when Tess had shown up at the dude ranch three days ago with a steely glare for Sam and a box of tissues in the car for Lorelei.

After the two women had left, Tess had asked quietly, "You want to talk about it?" At Lorelei's emphatic head shake, Tess had sighed. "For what it's worth, I'm sorry I encouraged you to make a move."

I'm not. Which was the problem in a nutshell. She didn't regret what had happened with Sam. In fact, she craved more. Whereas he was backpedaling so fast that he could have biked the annual Hill Country 600 in reverse.

Tess had promised to stay in touch and maybe even visit Lorelei—and Oberon—in Philadelphia. The cat was not happy about his current location in the carrier.

"Thank you for everything, Tess. I owe you."

"Are you kidding? After you spent all yesterday afternoon working on my taxes? I should name my firstborn after you!"

Ugh. So that a jaded man could one day accuse said firstborn of luring men to their dooms? "Let's just call it a draw."

Ava shuffled her feet. "Guess we should be going, huh?" But she didn't move toward her car. Instead, she remained in place, clutching her keys and scanning the street every few seconds.

He's not coming, Ava. Sam had already said goodbye, more or less. When she'd told him after the trail ride that she was going back to town with Tess, he'd nodded. "Probably a good idea," he'd said with no inflection whatsoever in his voice. The only time she'd seen him since was at the lawyer's office when paperwork for the inn had been handled. Afterward, he'd nodded to her and told her to take "real good care" of herself and the cat. And the jerk had actually sounded more choked up about the cat.

The B and B was officially hers now. And she was giving it away. She cast one last glance at the building, trying not to feel guilty. As if she were abandoning the place.

"Come on," she told Ava. "I'm ready." Which wasn't true, but it sounded better than *let's get the hell out of Dodge before I fall apart.*

As she climbed into the car, she felt an unexpected spark of kinship with her mother. Lorelei had been frustrated by her mom's seeming inability to move on after her husband's death, but Wanda had shared years of marriage and a child with the man she loved. All Lorelei had spent with Sam was a couple of weeks, some unexpectedly heartfelt confidences and the best sex of her life. Yet it felt as if she were leaving her heart in Texas. Would *she* be able to move on?

* * *

If Lorelei heard "good to have you back" from one more person, she was going to scream. She knew her coworkers at the insurance company meant well, but all they'd been doing for the past week was reminding her that it *didn't* feel good to be back.

She was trying to have a good attitude. It just wasn't working out very well. On her first day in, she'd dropped by Celia's office with a cookie basket to thank her for all the extra work she'd done in Lorelei's absence. She'd had half-formed plans of inviting the woman to have dinner sometime.

But she'd never issued the invitation because Celia had acted really weird, skittish even, glancing from Lorelei to the door as if considering making a run for it. Then she'd refused the cookies.

"If I ate stuff like that, I wouldn't be a size four." That had been the only time during the strange encounter her gaze settled on Lorelei, as if noting that Lorelei was categorically not a four.

Big deal, she'd found herself thinking. *My body looks great.* She knew this because Sam had told her, in various ways, about a hundred times in a forty-eight-hour window. She'd almost smiled at the memory until she realized that she wasn't supposed to be thinking about Sam Travis, much less grinning over him like a schoolgirl with a crush.

Lorelei had hoped that throwing herself into her job would distract her, but she wasn't getting her usual satisfaction out of it. As she looked at trends and calculated the odds of disaster, she felt annoyed. Was it healthy to spend so much time expecting the worst? Sure, being prepared was smart, but why were people always bracing themselves for bad things? If there were a thirty percent chance of something horrible happening, didn't that leave a seventy percent chance that it wouldn't? *Maybe we should play those odds for a change.*

She was sitting at her desk reevaluating her career on Thursday evening when her phone buzzed and Rick told her he was in the lobby.

"Can I come up?" he'd asked. "I haven't seen you since your trip." The only contact they'd had at all was when he'd emailed to tell her that those event tickets had fallen through, so never mind.

"Sure." She couldn't say she'd missed him, but he'd certainly never done anything to warrant her being bitchy. They could be friends.

Moments later, he strolled into her office, every bit as debonair as she remembered. Not a hair out of place, not a smudge of lint on his expensive suit. *Boring.*

"Lorelei." His voice was grave. "How *are* you? Holding up okay?"

If he'd been that worried, he could have called her.

"I'm fine." It wasn't strictly true, but it was a concise answer.

"Good. Look, Lorelei, my reasons for being here are twofold. First, I wanted to check on your well-being, of course."

Mental eye roll. "Of course."

"But I also felt I should discuss our relationship with you. You know we've always been free to see other people?"

"Mmm." She made a vague sound of agreement, trying not to remember just how much she'd seen of another man.

Rick linked his fingers behind his back, pacing in front of her as if her desk were the jury box. "I don't want this to be awkward for you, Lorelei. It certainly wasn't planned—"

"Rick." Her lips twitched and she wasn't sure if she was feeling more amusement or impatience. *Cut to the chase already.* "Are you trying to tell me you've found someone?" *Because, no offense, but she's welcome to you.*

He nodded, looking pained for a second. "And she works here. You know my gym is just around the corner? It turns out she goes there, too. Celia Warren?"

Is that why Celia had acted so squirrelly? Maybe the woman had felt guilty, stepping into Lorelei's shoes at work and then going out with a man Lorelei sometimes dated. *Good grief. She's Lorelei 2.0.*

"I think that's terrific news," Lorelei said sincerely. "You and Celia have a lot in common. Enjoy each other! Now, if you'll excuse me, I was about to head home and feed my cat."

Rick's forehead crinkled into perplexed lines. "You're not a cat person."

"That's okay, he's probably not technically a cat. More demon spawn than feline," she said with a fond smile. She should go home and see what Oberon had destroyed today. Yesterday, he'd knocked a glass award off the bookshelf. The day before, he'd shredded a roll of toilet paper into confetti. Prior to that, he'd hacked up a fur ball in her bathroom but hadn't actually mangled anything. Oberon liked to mix it up, keep things fresh.

When she'd squirted him with a water gun last night for clawing at the curtains, she'd threatened, "Watch it, or I'll mail you to Sam. And I might not poke holes in the box lid." A laughable threat on many levels. And Sam the nomad probably didn't even have a mailing address.

As she crossed the parking garage to her car, she wondered if Sam missed her at all. *Probably misses the cat.* And why not? Sometimes people who had trouble relating to others did better with animals. Look at how good he was with horses!

A horse wasn't likely to abandon you for a better barn or dump you on an estranged relative and never come back.

Lorelei told herself that thoughts like these were a dead end. It didn't matter if part of her sympathized with *why* Sam felt safer without any attachments. He, by his own choice, was no longer part of her life. But just as her car sat stuck in traffic, her mind seemed stuck on him. Everyone he'd cared about, including Wanda, had either died or left him. *Like me and the cat.* Assuming that he'd cared about her.

But she knew he did, whether he'd admitted it or not. He'd been candid with her about his past and about his fears. That couldn't have been easy for a man who had trouble trusting others. And he'd liked her enough to let his guard down at times, laughing with her and making her laugh. She still believed that Sam had a lot to offer a woman.

Unfortunately, he didn't see it that way. *Maybe because no one's ever tried to show him.* Lorelei bit her lip. Had she given up too easily? Where was the determination that had gotten her into a highly selective college and earned her ACAS?

Oberon met her at the door when she got home. He flopped on his back and yowled pitifully. She looked around but her preliminary search didn't find any new destruction. He followed her from room to room, meowing and sounding unhappy.

She scooped him into her arms and petted him. After a moment of token resistance, he stopped squirming and let himself enjoy it. Although he wouldn't give her the satisfaction of hearing it, she felt certain he was purring on the inside.

But as soon as she set him down so that she could look through the day's mail, he began complaining again. Lorelei shook her head. "You don't like it much here, do you? Want to know a secret? I'm not sure I do, either." Philadelphia had served a purpose in her life, had been a refuge, her method of running away.

How could she stay mad at Sam for fleeing emotional complications when she'd done the same thing for so long?

"Maybe," she told the cat, "it's time we call our real-estate agent."

"Hey, Travis!"

Sam turned on his bar stool to acknowledge a man he knew from his rodeo days, Bryan Wilton.

"Caught you in the shootout today," Bryan said as he took the seat next to Sam.

Sam was currently in Burnet, Texas, for their April festival. As part of the entertainment, tourists were treated to an old-fashioned bank robbery where the sheriff and his deputy chased thieves on horseback and justice prevailed in the end. Sam had first been offered the part of deputy, but these days he felt more like a bad guy, so he'd gone with that.

"Knew you were good with horses," Bryan said. "But I didn't know you could act."

"Oh, I'm quite the actor," Sam said, wondering if only he heard the self-loathing in his voice.

Those last couple of days Lorelei had been in Texas, he'd acted like he didn't give a damn. He figured that was better than a messy goodbye where he admitted he didn't want her to go. Part of him had wanted to hold on to her, but he knew that wouldn't last. Either she would have resented how little he had to offer and eventually dumped him or he would have bolted, his natural aversion to committing himself to one person or place too ingrained to overcome.

"So what are you up to these days?" Sam asked as the other man signaled the bartender. "Still on the rodeo circuit?"

Bryan shook his head. "No, I'm managing a tack shop now. I needed something more stable before I could convince my girl to marry me."

Sam almost spluttered beer. "You're married?"

"Engaged." Bryan beamed. "And couldn't be happier. I know, I know, I said it would never happen, but I just hadn't met the right woman yet. You'll see! One day you'll meet someone and it will change you."

He already had. And it had definitely

changed him. Oh, in most ways, he was still the restless loner he'd always been. But now he was painfully aware of what he was missing.

Working trail rides after the festival shootout was a difficult transition. Sam found that blasting at people—with fake guns, of course—suited his current mood more than being patient with tourists who had signed themselves up for three hours on horseback even though they seemed to have no knowledge whatsoever of riding. *Gonna have to take it really slow today.* Thank God this was just an afternoon jaunt and not one of the overnight trips.

A stable hand named Dave was helping check riders in and compiling all the signed forms. Two other stable hands were introducing guests to their mounts. Sam had been checking on the horses and equipment to make sure everything was in working order. Against his will, he remembered that ride with Lorelei when she'd asked with wide eyes if he had any idea of everything that could go wrong.

For a woman who'd been so preoccupied with accidental injury, how had she not understood the hazards just her smile posed? Sam had been falling for her before they ever left the B and B, but once he'd seen her astride a horse, out in the sunshine, grinning at him, he—

"Yo, Travis!" Dave snapped his fingers. "Did you hear me?"

"Sure," Sam lied.

Dave leaned against a stall door, smirking. "But, uh, just in case I misheard, maybe you should say it again."

"I just checked in a woman for the ride who asked to speak with you personally. She's at the front of the barn. Guess she has some questions about the trail."

Sam sighed, telling himself that even if the questions turned out to be an affront to common sense, he'd answer them patiently. He couldn't take his black mood out on every random stranger.

But as he blinked against the sunlight that backlit her, he realized this was not a stranger. His chest constricted painfully. "What are you doing here?" In his mind, he was screaming the question. Thankfully it came out as a whisper others wouldn't overhear.

Lorelei fisted her hands on her denim-clad hips, raising her chin in challenge. "I think you meant to say, 'Hi, Ms. Keller, nice to see you again.'"

Nice? That was the most asinine description he'd ever heard. It was incredible to see her again, to look into those dark eyes that had haunted his dreams—and, let's face it, most of his waking moments. But having her this close to him also hurt like breaking a rib or getting kicked in the gut, knocking the breath out of him as pain radiated through his body.

"I've signed up for today's ride," she informed him, as if this were an everyday event.

"You should be in Philadelphia."

"That would make my commute a little difficult. Hard to run my bed-and-breakfast from there."

"You took over the B and B?"

She couldn't do that to him! While Fredericksburg may not be his permanent home, he spent time there regularly. Now just driving past the town would be a torment.

Lorelei continued as if blithely unaware that he was in hell. "I'm not using my mom's theme, of course. I'll have to come up with something new. Between that and opening my own bookkeeping service, I should stay pretty busy."

"Sounds like," he managed to spit out. "I wish you all the best with everything."

Her eyes narrowed, sparks of anger beginning to show through her composure. "Oh, no. I've already heard that brush-off, the one where you tell me to take care and have a nice life. If you want to be rid of me this time, you'll have to come up with something more original. Otherwise…"

Otherwise?

How could one word sound so ominous yet conversely make his heart kick into an excited rhythm? Some foreign emotion welled within him, and Sam ruthlessly tamped it down. "I'm not sure what you mean."

"Then I'll spell it out for you. I am fighting for us. Because *you,*" she said, jabbing him in the chest with her finger, "are too much of a… How would you cowboys put it? A lily-livered coward. If you won't put it on the line for us, then I will."

He wasn't angered by her old-fashioned insult, but the truth in her sentiment infuriated him. Dammit, he *knew* he was scared, had warned her of that. Eventually, his negative feelings would sabotage their relationship, assuming something else hadn't first. People broke up with each other every day for a million different reasons, and a lot of those people were better adjusted than he was.

But instead of voicing any of that, he said as calmly as possible, "There is no 'us,' Lorelei."

"Well, there's gonna be," she declared. "Because we love each other. Not being together is just plain stupid."

That strange emotion surged again, like a river flooding its banks, and he identified the feeling this time. *Hope.* Hope he hadn't asked for and didn't want. "What is with you stubborn Fredericksburg females?" he growled. "First Barbara stalking me, now you?"

Her cheeks flushed, but she didn't rise to the taunt. She merely shook her head. "I'm not like Barbara. I'm being like my mom, all those times she called me last month and the month before that. I'm being persistent when it comes to someone I love."

He flinched at her use of the word. She truly loved him?

"I wish I'd given in to Mom," she said softly, "that I'd visited her more, tried harder while I still had the chance. You're going to wish that, too, Sam. If you let me leave here today, you'll regret it."

"So what's the alternative?" he asked her hoarsely. "The way I see it, no matter what happens, there will be regrets." He'd rather get them over with now than in a year, a decade. "You're the one who told me people should make more decisions with their heads, not with their hearts. That they should calculate the risks and protect themselves accordingly. You can't guarantee a happily ever after."

She ducked her gaze and he thought he might have won the argument by using her own reasoning. But when she looked up, he could see there was still plenty of fight left in her expression. He had an out-of-body moment where he almost wanted to grin because he felt proud of her.

"There is one guarantee," she protested. "You've heard the line about death and taxes? Nobody lives forever, Sam, and you and I both know life can be short. We've lost people close to us. Is this what they would have wanted for you? You're the most extroverted hermit I know. Even in a crowd of tourists, you're alone. If your life came to an end tomorrow, would you be satisfied with the way you spent it?"

No. God, no. He wanted to spend about a million more hours in her arms. He didn't need an impressive corporate career or social prestige or fancy belongings. He was beginning to think he needed Lorelei, though.

She reached up to caress the side of his face, her touch like a brand. "I won't stalk you, Sam. But if you decide love is worth the risk, you know where to find me." She gave him one last long look before walking out of the barn.

"Dude." At the sound of Davc's incredulous voice, Sam turned and realized that at some point during the conversation, they'd garnered an audience. "You're not just gonna let her go?"

Was he? Lorelei had told him repeatedly that she didn't believe in fairy tales. Neither did he. But he knew lots of cowboy legends, and very few of them ended happily.

Then have the courage to write your own damn story, Travis.

A wide-eyed middle-aged woman standing next to Dave made shooing motions with her hands. "Go after her, son. Before she gets away!"

That spurred him into motion as no other words could have. Ever since the last time Lorelei had walked away, he'd felt like a husk of a man, going through the motions of his life with no real purpose or enjoyment. Could he endure that again?

He raced into the sunshine, quickly catching her. "Lorelei, wait!" He spun her around, hating himself for the tears that sparkled on her lashes. "Oh, hell, don't cry. I'm not worth it, darlin'."

She smacked him on the arm. "Yeah, you *are*. That's kind of the point."

"I love you." He blurted it fast before he could lose his nerve.

Her jaw dropped but she quickly regrouped, affecting a smug expression even though tears rolled down her face. "I told you so!"

His eyes felt suspiciously damp, too, and he pulled her against his chest so that she didn't see. "Know-it-all Ivy League pain-in-the-ass," he said affectionately. He smoothed his hand over her hair. "But I do love you."

She tilted her head back. "Love you, too."

Giving in to the emotions swamping him, Sam framed her face and captured her mouth with his. Applause and hoots of approval sounded behind them. Lorelei grinned against his lips but didn't move away. Their deep, thorough kiss felt like an unspoken vow. A promise of new beginnings and happy endings and, most important, being there for each other to weather everything in between.

* * * * *